AND BUSINESS IS GOOD

PROTECTED BY THE DAMNED, BOOK 3

MICHAEL TODD   MICHAEL ANDERLE
LAURIE STARKEY

DISRUPTIVE IMAGINATION®

AND BUSINESS IS GOOD

AND BUSINESS IS GOOD TEAM

Beta Readers

Bree Buras (Aussie Awesomeness)
Timothy Cox (The Myth)
Tom Dickerson (The man)
S Forbes (oh yeah!)
Dorene Johnson (US Navy (Ret) & DD)
Diane Velasquez (Chinchilla lady & DD)

JIT Readers

Tim Adams
Jim Caplan
John Ashmore
Sarah Weir
Daniel Weigert
Tim Bischoff
Paul Westman
Micky Cocker
Larry Omans
Joshua Ahles

If we missed anyone, please let us know!

Editor
Lynne Stiegler

*To Family, Friends and
Those Who Love
To Read.
May We All Enjoy Grace
To Live The Life We Are
Called.*

There was a moment—just one moment—where everything stood still. Where the bubbling of the lava streams, the screeching of the tormented, and the agony of the Damned all paused.

T'Chezz stepped forward into the light of the flaming torches, his lips trembling in anger. He slashed his claws across the chest of the human that hung from the ceiling, and blood rolled down its skin. Then everything went back to normal, whatever *that* was. No, that wasn't right…there was more anger in the room than there had been before.

"You are useless," T'Chezz spat as blood dripped to the stone floor beneath his clawed hooves.

The hanging human's arms and ankles pulled him in separate directions, and the shreds of his torn clothing drooped from his bleeding and battered body.

He had been sucked down into the bowels of hell and chained for T'Chezz's pleasure. Unable to handle the burning of his wounds, he whimpered, then tried to speak.

But fear clogged his throat.

"You are *pathetic*," T'Chezz growled, pointing his grotesque fingers at the man. "You are *Chosen*—you should be able to withstand a little torture. It would all be over if you just told the truth!"

"I'm…trying," the man gargled. His stomach seemed to be filled with half his blood, and the other half was trying to seep out of his mouth.

"Oh, you are?" T'Chezz said, moving over to him with demonic speed.

He squeezed the man's chin forcefully and snarled in his face as sweat poured from the human's skin. The demon rolled his eyes in disgust and shook his head, then turned and walked across the room.

He looked out over the bubbling molten rivers that ran through the underground inferno.

T'Chezz smiled, running his fingers sensually over the array of tools on his desk. "If you won't say it, then maybe I'll have to cut it out of you."

"NO!" The man panicked, straining against his chains. "*Please.*"

"Oh, *please*," T'Chezz mimicked, picking up a small blade and laughing. "No need to beg, since it won't make any difference." He looked at the politician. "Don't you know that politicians are the worst of evils?" He noted the man's disbelief. "It's true. Perhaps not in the first generation—usually that group tossed out their ineffectual and useless predecessors. I am referring to the fuckers who have been screwing up the government *lately*."

T'Chezz laughed loudly as he walked back to the

hapless human, then casually stabbed the blade into the politician's leg.

The politician screamed in pain, closing his eyes. His perfect hair was no longer perfect, his pressed suit was in tatters, and his adoring constituents were far above him. T'Chezz pulled the knife back out and wiped it across his tongue, then shook his head.

"Your blood is poison," he spat.

The politician groaned as T'Chezz's bellowing laughter echoed through the room. His head was down and his eyes were shut tightly, but when he unclenched his muscles he noticed the pain was gone. Slowly he opened his eyes and looked down at his now-free and clothed body. Even his shoes were still freshly polished.

He stared at his hands and turned them over as he shrugged the five-thousand-dollar suit jacket up on his shoulders. He was sweating, shaking with fear, but his body was unscathed. He didn't know if he had been healed, or if all of it had just been in his head.

"These hunters are closing in," the human said in a shaky voice.

"Then maneuver," T'Chezz told him. His back was to the politician. "You are the perfect plant in their world. They trust you because of your power."

"They fear me, which is different than trust," he tried to explain.

"Better," T'Chezz corrected. "Fear is what drives the human race. Fear is what I see in their eyes as they stare into the darkness, clutching their sacred books and whispering their prayers. Fear is behind it all, but until now they had no idea what they feared."

He looked out the window. "That will change."

"What do you want me to do?" the man asked.

"Your job," T'Chezz growled, turning back to the politician. "I will place you back on Earth, but you are expected to do better; perform better. I can promise you that your being a valuable plant will be completely irrelevant if you don't."

"I understand." The politician trembled.

"You'd better," T'Chezz snapped. "I will eat your flesh myself, and you don't smell appetizing at all."

"It will be done." The politician grimaced.

"See that it is," T'Chezz said, walking toward the door. "It's time these humans understand that we were on Earth first. We don't need their meatbags walking around."

"Where are you going?" the politician yelled, cowering as T'Chezz snapped his head toward him.

"To meet my new partner." He smiled, his fangs dripping. "I'm hungry, and not just for flesh. I'm hungry to get this started. I won't sit around and allow these Damned to get in the way. This is *my* time, politician. This is *my* world, and these humans—these 'killers,' as you like to call them— they will learn who their real master is. It's not a man in a suit on the top of the hill. They will wish for scumbags like you when I am through with them. They will wish for death even before that. *Go!*"

T'Chezz threw his hand in the air and stomped out of the room, leaving the politician thinking about what to do next. He closed his eyes, feeling the heat and swirling air around him. When he opened them again he was back on the surface, only this time things were different. His existence and survival hinged on what came next.

No more screwups allowed.

———

"Seriously, I think Jessica has slept with the entire cast," Eric confided.

"Even the old maid, Mrs. Avers?" Katie chuckled.

"*ESPECIALLY* Mrs. Avers." Eric shook his head, sadly. "She even did her dust wand. Bitch is dirty under that maid costume—don't act like you don't see it.

"That is so gross." Katie shook her head. "*Days of Long Since Past* is like the ultimate in soap operas, which means pretty much everyone is a whore."

"I wish life worked that way," Derek chimed in, staring at the television.

"I don't know," Eric said. "I don't think Korbin is interested, and you know Katie over here gets her rocks off with swords and pushups."

"Hey," Katie said, pouting. "I am more than that."

Both guys looked at her and raised their eyebrows. She shook her head and turned back to focus on the show, but she could feel their stares. She started to laugh.

"All right, fine…maybe not that much different than what you are saying," Katie admitted. "Still, it's nice to think that I am not any of those characters. They all sleep with each other. It's like this twisted circle of friends."

"That circle would be more like a tree if it were like that here." Derek laughed. "Katie at the top, with many branches."

"Right," Katie said, "which is why I keep my tree branchless right now."

"This show saved lives once." Eric wasn't listening to the other two—or chose not to get involved in the great tree debate.

"Bullshit," Derek argued. "How?"

"No, I'm serious." Eric turned to them. "My squadron was out in the Sandpit and we were in this firefight. It was freaking intense, man…seriously. There were injured; we had been fighting for hours, and everyone was freaking exhausted. They had us pinned down too, like bad. We were in the city, stuck in this half-blown-to-hell building surrounded on all sides by these fucktards. I seriously figured that was it for us—we were done."

"So how did the soap opera help you?" Derek leaned forward.

"Well, after hours upon hours of hiding and shooting and hiding and shooting, we were at a standstill," Eric said. "There was this raw recruit…his name was Johns, and he was in charge of tactical over the wire. You know, 'our eye on the ground' kind of thing. Anyway, he came over the net and told us that we had thirty minutes to get out of there or risk missing that day's show. Shit, all of us had been wondering whether Jessica had slept with Ivan or not, and they were supposed to reveal the truth on that day's episode. It was a really big deal for us."

"So what happened?" Katie asked, wide-eyed.

"Well, the sheer amount of lead we threw in the next thirty minutes probably cost the US government close to fifty K." He chuckled. "But in the end we nailed the other side. They never even saw it coming. It was like a Hail Mary out of nowhere. There wasn't one of us who didn't get a hot casing in our boot or down the back of our shirt, but it was fucking amazing. None of our men ended up getting hurt after the start of the firefight."

"Did you get to see the show?" Derek asked excitedly.

"Hell yeah, we did." Eric nodded. "We hauled ass out of there, and only missed the opening credits. Jessica didn't end up sleeping with Ivan, and the whole damn platoon sat there cheering and booing from the MWR tent. Was probably one of my best moments out there. We felt *real* again, you know? Like we were more than our guns. We were enjoying something that everyone at home was enjoying too. It made us feel normal, even if it was for only a minute."

"Did you have many fights after that?"

"Right after that was one of the bloodiest battles we had ever seen," he said, his eyes glazing over. "We lost thirty-two souls that day, and not one of us saw that day's soap."

"The sergeant stopped being an ass after that." Eric chuckled. "He hadn't been too happy with all the paperwork from the first battle. I'd do it again, though. It was nice feeling like a person again."

"I hear you there," Katie said, glancing at Derek. "I hear you."

When the soap opera was over, Katie clapped her hands and shook her head. It was always exciting. She sat there in the chair for a moment while Eric flipped through the channels. All of them had a day off for the most part, so she really had nowhere to rush off to.

"You want to watch some baseball with us?" Eric asked,

looking at her. "There's a doubleheader."

Katie held back a smirk while Pandora pretended to gag and puke in her mind.

"No, I think I'm gonna put some real clothes on and actually get some work done," she told him. "Maybe next time."

"All right," he said. "We'll be here."

Katie got up from the chair she was lounging in and stretched, then walked away without any more discussion. It wasn't that she didn't like sports—she had been an athlete in her former life—but baseball was about as exciting to her as watching grass grow. Instead, she changed her clothes and headed over to Joshua's building to see how their efforts were going.

She leisurely walked outside and across the sand to the gate, which was already open, then went inside and down the main stairs. Joshua was sitting behind his desk staring down at two knives, and he looked up and smiled at Katie when she walked in.

"H-hey," he said, standing up and holding out the knives. "Perfect timing. I finished these two knives for you."

"Oh, great!" Katie chirped, taking them from him.

They were just as beautiful as the others, with shimmering metal, perfectly made handles, and steel butts. Joshua reached out and turned the knife blade-down, then tapped on the butt. Almost as if it had been magically inscribed, two cursive Ks vibrated with color. Katie ran her finger over the letters and smiled as she looked up at Joshua.

"You haven't given me a name yet, so I put two K's for

Korbin's Killers," he told her.

"How did you..."

"Hang out here long enough, you learn a thing or two." He chuckled, rubbing his hands together. "I'm really excited, though, that I'm able to cut my time down. I have been getting two knives a week done with this new machinery, which is more than I have ever done before. I know you wanted an increase in productivity, but so far this is the best I can do."

"These are great," Katie exclaimed. "I know these take time to make. It's not an overnight process. How are you with the bullet idea?"

"At the moment?" he said, pulling out some papers. "Not very far with the idea at all. I am trying to figure out some technical things. The intrinsic energy of the metal is hard to control. I can't just turn it off and on, and I'm trying to figure out how to melt it down without losing the metal's properties. It's beyond anything I can look up, and when these books my father left behind were written there was nothing even remotely similar to bullets. On top of that, even if I melt the metal down, I'm trying to figure out how I would spray the molten liquid."

"Can you not just mold them into bullets?" Katie asked.

"No. Bullets aren't a solid form like you are thinking, not with the energy involved," Joshua replied.

She laughed. "This is all a bit above my paygrade. Just keep working on it. I'm sure it will come to you eventually. They are important, but I don't want production of other things to slow down either."

"Right. I'll keep working at it."

"Great." Katie smiled. "I'll check back in later."

Katie walked back upstairs, slightly disappointed. When she reached the top, Mamacita looked over her shoulder and smiled as she accepted an order from FedEx. She checked the boxes in, signed for them, and closed the door as Katie walked over.

"Hey," Katie greeted her. "What are you doing here?"

"I thought Joshua might need some help, and I dropped him off this morning so he didn't keep parking that huge van in the driveway." She looked Katie up and down. "You okay? You look tired."

"I'm okay." Katie sighed. "Just trying to get through the days and keep the business going. How are the girls?"

"They are all very good." The madam smiled. "They ask about you and Joshua all the time. I have allowed some of them to come here with me and help out when needed."

"Nice!" Katie smiled. "All right, I'm going to head into the office. If you need anything from me, you know where to find me."

"Take a nap," Mamacita called, picking up a box and walking carefully across the stone floor in her heels.

Katie shook her head and walked over to the office, plopping down in the new chair. She sighed and looked around for a moment, then opened the books. As she looked down at the numbers, her heart sank slightly in her chest.

They had already spent a shit-ton of money.

Even with the infusion of capital from Korbin, she was going to have to start offsetting the costs—and she had no idea how to do that. The company was going to run out of resources, and that meant they weren't going to make as many weapons as they needed.

2

Katie dragged her feet through the doors and into the main building. The last thing she wanted to do was go to Korbin and tell him about the issues with the company, but she didn't have any choice. They needed to get things under control or they would be up Shit Creek with no way to make the weapons, much less create a viable business out of it.

She had gone through too much already to get the company going, and she wasn't going to chicken out now.

When she reached Korbin's office, she knocked on the open door.

"Katie," he said, shuffling some paperwork as he looked up at her. "What can I do for you?"

"I wanted to see if you had a minute to talk about the company."

"Not right now." He shook his head. "I have to jump on a conference call with the other team leaders. I'll call you when I'm available."

"Thanks."

She closed the door behind her as she left and headed back up to the main area, smiling kindly to Damian as she passed his quarters. She didn't feel like talking with anyone else, and she wanted to put the new knives in a package for Korbin.

She figured if she was going to go to him for a favor, she should probably take something as a peace offering.

Or bribe.

"Katie," Calvin called from behind her, "you got a package from eBay."

Oooh, what is it? Pandora asked excitedly.

"Thanks," Katie turned and walked back, picking the package up from the table.

She turned without a word to Pandora or the others and took it back up to her room. When she got inside with the door shut she set the knives down on the dresser and opened the package, pulling an old dusty book from the wrappings.

It was a historical book, one that was over two hundred years old. Katie had found it on eBay and hoped it would give her some more information on what she was facing.

What do you want that thing for? Pandora sniffed.

I want to see if it has any more information on the Seventy-Two, Katie answered. *I want to know what I will be facing in the coming days, especially with your brother on the hunt for my meat sack, or so you keep calling it.*

I don't know why you don't just come to me, Pandora said. *I can tell you all about them if you would just ask.*

Could I really believe you? Katie asked. *You don't have the best record of telling me the truth and this is too important for me to have doubts.*

Point taken, Pandora said.

There are two ways I can look at this, Katie said. *I can trust that your boost alone is enough to kill him, or I can assume that it is going to take more than that to keep my body safe. I have to go with the latter of the two, especially since my soul is depending on it. I don't want to be wrong about this, you know? I want to be able to feel comfortable that I can run into this T'Chezz character at any point and know I can handle myself with him.*

I get it, Pandora said. *How about I do this: I won't give you any information, but I will tell you if the book is wrong on something. It's much worse to face an enemy you think you know about and be wrong than to have no idea. If you know nothing, you will be open to whatever happens.*

All right, Katie said. *That sounds like an acceptable deal.*

Katie got up from the bed and walked over to the dresser, putting the book down and opening it to the first page. She grabbed the two knives off the table and started to box them up. Carefully she wrapped each knife in tissue paper and placed them, one on top of the other, inside of the box.

She didn't want to be too girlie about it, but she wanted it to look as nice as possible since she was going to pretty much be asking for something in return. She glanced over at the first page of the book and skipped through until it reached the part about the seventy-two.

So, the first demon they talk about is Asmodeus, Katie said.

Oh, lord, Pandora giggled.

It says here that Asmodeus is the orgy devil of sensuality, Katie said, a slight blush on her cheeks. *It is said he is also immensely spiteful and protective of his lovers. It says that he uses his allure, his sexual allure, to bring his victims to him. Some he keeps as sexual slaves of sorts and the others are usually enemies or blood lust.*

Asmodeus is definitely alluring, that's for damn sure. Pandora snickered. *He is like the ultimate ladies' man, and I've had my fair share of fun with him. Not so much with his asshole tendencies, but I digress.*

Okay. Katie sighed. *So, he is the most charming being I could ever meet but, in the end he will swallow me whole.*

After you swallow him, Pandora agreed.

Enough! Katie interrupted. *I get the picture. So, beware of any romantic or lustful feelings I may have toward someone. Got it. Noted.*

It would be the most passionate feeling you have ever felt, Pandora said. *Like your shit is on fire or something.*

That sounds like what you get when you sleep with one of the guys from the pub, Katie said, amused by her joke.

Humans are weird, Pandora groaned. *Okay, who is next?*

Before Katie could move forward Korbin came over the loudspeaker, calling her to his office. She finished up with the box of knives and closed the book, stashing it in the top drawer of her dresser.

I guess we will pick this up later, Katie said. *After I sell my soul to another kind of devil.*

Korbin sat at his desk waiting for Katie to come down, wondering what she wanted to talk about. He could tell by the tepidness in her voice when she first came to his office that she didn't want to be there to talk about whatever it was bothering her.

He looked up as Katie came out of the elevator and walked toward his now open door.

"Hey," he said. "Have a seat."

"Thanks." She sat down. "I brought you something."

He watched as she pulled a box from her lap, which was tied closed with a ribbon.

He took it from her and smiled, pulling the bow off slowly and carefully lifting the lid. He stared down at the blue tissue paper and carefully picked up the two pieces, unwrapping each separately.

Inside, there were a pair of very beautiful knives, hand crafted by Joshua, with the same glimmering texture to them. He could already imagine himself using them on a demon.

"These are very expensive knives, as you are probably aware," Katie said.

"Yeah." Korbin nodded, shaking his head. "They are beautiful. Joshua does amazing work. I am glad to see that he has been able to sit down and get some work done."

"Me too," she said. "That being said, I think I need some help—*your* help—with the business."

"Me?" he said, putting down the knives and leaning back in his chair. "What's going on? What's the issue?"

"Well, I looked at the books this morning, and to be frank, we are hemorrhaging money," Katie explained. "I guess between the start of the company, training, and this new threat that just seems to be growing with the infected, I haven't been paying the kind of attention to what Joshua is doing as I should be."

"All right," Korbin said, pulling his eyebrows together. "What kind of help are you looking for?"

"I just need someone to go over the books," Katie replied. "To make sure everything is being done as efficiently as possible. We all know there are always places we can trim expenses, and I need to know where we can do that with what we are ordering and paying out for. I may have knowledge, but I lack experience in this area and I think that you could help—and not be too intimidating to Joshua at the same time."

"Are we sure we can trust Joshua?"

"Yes," Katie said, nodding. "Definitely. The thing is, he is doing what he thinks needs to be done, but he is a blade maker. He isn't a businessman in any sense of the word. I'm sure he orders just like he assumes he should. I doubt if he knows that everything is negotiable with the quantity of supplies we are ordering, for example,."

"All right, I understand." Korbin rubbed his chin. "So basically, he goes in and orders whatever he needs to perform his job, most likely from the same people he ordered from before. He assumes the price is the price, and that is it."

"That is what I believe," Katie admitted. "I also worry that he won't know how to handle profits, not that we have any right now. I don't think he will understand that profits need to be distributed among different sectors of the company. He will most likely just put that money back into supplies, like a vicious circle."

"And we will continue to think we are operating at cost." Korbin nodded. "Where do you keep your books?"

"Right now there is only one. The guys built me an

office on the main floor of the building next door, and I keep them in there so Joshua has access to them when he does all his ordering and accepting of packages."

"Do you think he can be trained, or do you think we will have to have someone else do the negotiations and ordering?" Korbin asked.

Katie thought for a moment. "Probably the latter," she finally answered. "He is a good kid, but he has serious social anxiety. I think trying to push him to negotiate with these suppliers—some who are really pushy—will only make things worse for him, and therefore for us."

"Right," Korbin said. "Okay. Sure, I'll look at the books with you."

"Thank you, Korbin. And you don't have to wait for me to be there—just whenever you are available. During the day the office is open, and at night just grab the key from me or Joshua if he is still there. I really appreciate this."

"Not a problem," Korbin said, glancing at Eric in the pit below them. "Why don't you suit up and go work out with Eric. He has been going at it for hours."

"Absolutely." She nodded, then got up and walked to the door. "And thanks again."

Korbin just smiled, feeling good about helping her out.

Eric could feel the sweat rolling down his forehead as he pushed the weights over his head and lowered again.

He growled as he pushed back up. The muscles in his arms and back quaked under the pressure. He didn't know if it had anything to do with the demon inside him but he felt damn strong now, ready to take on whatever the fuck came his way.

He was pumped to be Damned, pumped that he could use the same sick sons of bitches that killed his comrades to kill the aforementioned sons of bitches. He was pumped to have that extra boost, but he wouldn't misuse it.

"You are looking buff." Katie was leaning against the wall. "Don't overdo it, or you will hurt yourself."

"I feel amazing," Eric replied, glancing at her. "Like I could tackle a bull."

"Wait till it starts talking to you all the time." Katie chuckled. "You just need to be careful, that's all. Its ultimate goal is take you over, and when that happens there is no going back. That's when we have to make a really hard choice."

"That won't happen." Eric racked the weights and stood up. "I'm tougher than that. I won't let it take me over."

Shit, there isn't even a very big demon in there. Pandora sniffed. *And the thing is terrified still—or maybe that's just because we showed up. Either way, the thing is not giving him anything extra, really.*

Let him be, Katie told her.

It's hard to ignore him. He has such a hard-on for you that you would think Asmodeus was inside him. Pandora chuckled. *His muscles are going to deflate, and we're gonna watch him spin around the room like a fucking skin balloon.*

Where do you come up with this shit? Katie asked. *"Skin balloon?"*

"You okay?" Eric waved a hand in front of her.

"Yeah," she said, shaking the far-off look from her face. "Just thinking, is all."

"Yeah, well, you aren't going to be the only badass in here for long," he told her. "Not that the others aren't awesome, but it's obvious who takes care of shit."

"That's not true," Katie said. "We all have our special skills. If it were true, Korbin and Jeremy wouldn't have saved that school bus full of kids."

"Oh, agreed," Eric said, wiping his forehead with a towel. "But there's definitely something different about *you*."

She nodded her agreement. "Yeah—I'm insane. Being on the team, running a business, and apparently checking in on you guys too. It's the voices in my head."

Damn right. Pandora snickered. *You could all use voices like mine in your damn heads.*

Like we need tumors, Katie shot back.

Did you just compare me to a growth? Pandora asked, wonder in her voice.

"Well," Katie said, clapping her hands together and ignoring Pandora. "You want to do some sparring?"

"Hell, yeah," Eric said, walking into the center of the pit. "I'll take it easy on you."

"Well, thanks." Katie chuckled.

They circled slowly around each other, both crouched in defensive positions. Katie watched the movements of his legs and arms. He stepped forward quickly and jabbed but Katie dodged, nodding her head as she slapped his hand aside.

Eric chuckled and tilted his head back and forth, stretching his neck.

Katie stepped forward, but leaned to the right when he

attempted to kick her in the chest. She grabbed his leg and spun him around, pushing him playfully.

"You are doing better." Katie laughed, bouncing up and down. "Just don't react too soon."

The two sparred for over an hour, Eric not once hurting Katie in the least. He almost had her down at one point, but she swept his legs and stood back up, laughing.

He was having fun with it…almost too much fun.

Katie knew he would be good for their team, but he would have to watch himself and not get too cocky.

When she was done there, she thanked him for a good workout and walked off toward weapons. She figured she and Calvin could end the day with some training in that area.

All the while, though, her mind was on the Seventy-Two. She wondered what else that book had to say.

3

T he sun was starting to go down as Katie sat on the edge of her bed, combing her hair after getting out of the shower.

She had worked on the bow and arrow with Calvin for the afternoon, figuring if Joshua could ever get the spray down they could put it on the arrows' heads. She thought it would probably be good to know how to use the weapons in the armory, especially since she now owned a weapons manufactory.

Either way. she would end up taking it out for a test drive in the coming days.

Katie looked at the book, but her stomach growled, letting her know just how hungry she was. The guys had picked up chicken and potato salad and such but what she was really in the mood for was some delicious Italian food.

She had been craving it for like a week, but hadn't really felt like going out with her normal babysitter.

Korbin never let her go anywhere alone unless she left

without telling him, which was a serious breach in the rules. Korbin had questioned her on occasion, and she didn't want to experience those occasions any more often than she already did.

Katie walked over to her closet and stood there a moment looking in, then pulled out some clothes.

She got dressed and pulled her hair back into a ponytail.

The desire for Italian wasn't going to go anywhere anytime soon, so she figured babysitter or not, that was her destination for dinner.

She left her room and made her way to Korbin's office, laughing at the guys as they chowed down on fried chicken. It wasn't often that they were all quiet at the same time, but with their mouths full they really had no choice.

Katie thought about messing with them, but her hunger for everything Italian had taken over like a storm.

She still couldn't figure out why she was so damn hungry in the first place.

Either way she wasn't going to sit around and be miserable, and the thought of fried chicken made her groan, so instead of saying anything she nodded at Calvin as she passed and climbed into the elevator. She leaned back against the wall as it took her down to the office, thinking about the book, the company, and everything that was going on. Her life was interesting; no one could take that away from her.

When she reached Korbin's office, he had his head down and was typing something with emotion. Katie leaned against the frame and cleared her throat. He looked up and stopped typing, sitting back and nodding permission for her to come in. She smiled and meandered into the office, looking around.

"How was training with Eric?" he asked.

"All right." Katie shrugged. "He thinks he is the fucking Hulk right now."

Korbin pursed his lips, considering her information. "Should we be worried?"

"Worried?" She shook her head. "No, but it wouldn't hurt to keep an eye on him. You don't want him to take stupid risks, and possibly get him or someone else killed. From what we can tell the demon inside him isn't very big, but if it really wants to take over it could make a move. If he doesn't dial his excitement at being Damned down just a bit, he could find himself on the opposite end of the stick."

"And that wouldn't be good at all." Korbin sighed. "Well, thanks for sparring with him. Now, what can I do for you?"

"I just wanted to let you know that I was going to go to Bootlegger Italian Bistro on Las Vegas Blvd, the south side. They have some good Italian food, and I am craving Italian horribly," Katie told him. "I figured I'd give you a heads-up, so you could send your spy after me while I was out. Unless you just want me to take him with me, like last time?"

"You are perceptive." Korbin shook his head. "But no, not this time. Go have your Italian. Be safe, enjoy. The guys are all having a great time up there with their mound of chicken."

"I know, I saw that," Katie replied, laughing. "And are you sure? I mean, you normally want me to have a nurse-maid. You know, with all those creepy people out there and how fragile I am, I could easily be pulled into a candy van."

"You could." He laughed, leaning back in his chair. "But I think I will go on faith here."

"Thanks, boss." She turned to leave.

"And a cannoli," he added.

"You know," Katie agreed, turning back around, "I think that for a little bit of freedom, a cannoli can be arranged. Any specific kind?"

"A traditional one." He laughed. "None of that fancy shit."

"Right. I'll make sure to order it that way. 'A cannoli—the traditional kind, with none of that fancy shit.'"

"Hey, I bet you that you wouldn't be the first person who said that in a restaurant," he surmised. "I grew up in an Italian household, so I tend to get a little picky about my cannolis."

"Now you're making me nervous." She chewed on her lip. "Will the cannoli be up to Korbin's standards? If it's not, I just want to put out there that it is not only not my fault, I will not pay the punishment for it."

"Ehhhh," he said, squinting one eye, "all right. You drive a hard bargain, but that's fair. No cleanup duty for you if the cannoli sucks, but that doesn't mean I won't go to this restaurant just to give them a piece of my mind."

"Of course, boss."

Katie walked out of the office laughing and shaking her head. Some days Korbin could be the most intimidating man on Earth, but on other days he was quite enjoyable to be around.

She was well aware he had a lot of responsibilities, and they weren't just about keeping the house afloat.

He felt responsible for every human soul in that building, and every human soul outside the building. Katie finally understood what Damian had meant when they first met about Korbin's need to take care of the world being what would eventually kill him.

She was starting to agree with that statement whole-heartedly.

Katie rounded the corner into the garage and looked at the SUVs, which were parked in rows. She went over to the box on the wall and pulled out a set of keys for the one closest to the entrance. As she walked toward it Joshua climbed into Mamacita's car, and it headed out.

Katie smiled as the little red sports car blew down the driveway. She stood there for a moment holding the keys in her hand and thinking before turning around and walking back into the complex. She pushed herself hard, running back up the stairs two at a time to Korbin's office, and stood in his doorway breathing heavily.

"You forget something?" He glanced at her and raised an eyebrow. "Your lungs, perhaps?"

"Hold on," she said trying to catch her breath. "I have… a…question."

He chuckled. "All right. By all means! I'll wait."

She raised a middle finger. "Hey, don't be snappy, or you'll get a chocolate-chip-cookie-dough cannoli."

"Oh, God." He cringed.

She stood up. "So, I was downstairs in the garage, and I watched Mamacita drive off in her little red sports car with Joshua. And it got me thinking."

"About Mamacita, or little red sports cars?"

"Neither," Katie said, shaking her head and sitting down

in a chair in front of his desk. "Is there some kind of rule against me owning my own vehicle?"

"No."

"That's great!" She smiled and waved her arms. "I would totally be a lot less conspicuous driving around in my own car. I could park normally, and no one would look at me because I hopped out of a souped-up, blacked-out SUV."

"Yeah, sure." He slowly nodded his head. "Though I think the car dealer might look at you funny."

She froze. "Why?"

"Well, dead people don't usually buy cars." He shrugged.

Katie dropped her arms into her lap. "Shit."

"Not sure how you would get it licensed and pay for it," he continued.

"I'm legally dead." She put her hand over her eyes. "Which is why my bank account was closed and I had to start hoarding my money in my mattress like a doomsday person."

"Yep," he said.

"I'm glad I didn't go in there and question them." Katie rolled her eyes. "They would have thought I was insane. Well, all right. Never mind." She stood up.

"Sorry to burst your bubble," Korbin called as Katie walked out of his office.

As she walked back to the garage she wondered briefly why the Damned weren't issued new identities, but put it out of her mind in favor of getting some food into her stomach. She'd do something about it later—maybe start a revolution or something. She jumped in the SUV and headed over to Bootlegger, just happy to get some Italian in her. Sure, her bubble had been burst, but it wasn't the first time and it wouldn't be the last, either.

She parked the car and went inside, smiling at all the memories she had of going there years ago. On the inside the place was classy, with wooden accents, deep browns and reds in the carpet, and wallpaper she was sure was original from when they had first opened.

The waitress showed her into the bar and to the right, into a booth that had a picture of the Rat Pack on the wall. The small plaque above it talked about the members of the Rat Pack who had eaten in this booth so long ago.

The place was history. So many famous faces had gone through there, and still did. The first time she had gone, Celine Dion had come in with a couple of other people. She had almost died. They had a lounge area where there was live music, the bar, a dining area, and a club-like place on the other side that was fairly new.

The place where she was sitting was her favorite, though. She could watch everyone and eat delicious food at the same time.

It was the perfect choice for her, especially after all the stress she had been under. For an hour or two she could feel like a normal girl, not a demon-hunting Damned.

Katie smiled and looked down at the menu, her mouth already watering at the selections. There was the normal Italian you would find at restaurants like spaghetti, ravioli, and pizza, but then there was the stuff she loved to come there for.

The specialty salads, the manicotti, the steaks, and her personal favorite, the *Scaloppini di Lorraine*. She was pretty sure she could live there if they let her.

The problem at that point was deciding what exactly she wanted to get, and how much she could eat while still leaving room for tiramisu, which was her favorite dessert.

I want everything on this menu, Pandora said. *I mean, like,* everything.

Calm down, there. Katie chuckled.

I am dead serious here, woman. You have got to scratch my itch, Pandora grumped. *Why do you think that you were craving it as badly as you were? Now, we definitely have to have steak, the ravioli is a must, and your veal dish—sure, why not?*

Katie, for once, had to admit her insufficiency. *I can't eat that much.*

Why not? Pandora asked. *I'll just up your metabolism when you start to get full, and poof—you can eat more food. Now, what time does this place close? We have some serious culinary destruction to get working on.*

They don't close. Katie sipped her water. *They are open twenty-four hours a day, seven days a week.*

Pandora chuckled. *That should be enough time.*

Just don't kill me Seven style, Katie groaned.

What is that? Pandora asked.

It's this movie about a serial killer who kills people based on the seven deadly sins. One of the guys died due to gluttony, Katie explained.

That's brilliant, Pandora said. *Let me guess, they fed him to death?*

Yep, Katie replied. *His stomach burst.*

Oh, God, Pandora cringed. *That sounds like a delightfully terrible torture.*

Don't get all hell-demon on me at a time like this, Katie said. *And by the way, I had no idea that you liked Italian food.*

Are you kidding me? Pandora scoffed. *I spent almost half a century in Italy shacked up with this hot Italian demon, eating this little old lady's Italian cooking.*

The little old lady lived that long? Katie asked.

Well, when she was animated by two horny demons she did, Pandora replied. *That's not the point. The point is, I pretty much ate from sunup to sundown, and then through the night. As soon as you walked into this place I felt like I was back there on the green hills drinking wine, naked in the sun. The food here smells on-point.*

I love Italian too, but for a much less vibrant reason. Katie grabbed one of the small square bread pieces they served. *My dad brought me here when I was a little girl. He was Italian, or part-Italian. He loved this place, and because he loved it I did too. Seriously, I don't know why I haven't come here before now.*

It had been the first real thing the two of them had had in common. They both loved Italian food for oddly different reasons, but still…

When the waitress came to the table, she ordered two appetizers and an entrée to start.

Throughout the night the food poured in, plate after plate. The staff couldn't believe that a tiny thing like Katie could put down that amount of food. Pandora was true to her word, though; as soon as she started to feel the least bit full she would ramp up her metabolism, and suddenly she would be ready to eat all over again.

She didn't spend money like that often, but she figured there was nothing better to spend it on than wine and Italian food.

When they had tried everything on the menu that they wanted, they moved over to dessert. Luckily Katie was able to get Pandora to agree on a cannoli and tiramisu, and of course the cannoli to go for the boss man.

If she'd let Pandora have her way, Katie would have diabetes by the time she left the place. The staff were very friendly, and boxed up some food for her to take with her.

Katie paid the tab and tipped generously, feeling like she could barely carry her body out of the place at that point.

Her pants were digging into her stomach, and her head felt like it was full of marinara sauce. She had definitely outdone herself.

4

Damian walked into the living room and looked around. He nodded at Calvin, who was sitting on the couch drinking a bottle of water, then walked over to the window. From the padlock on the door of the company building, it was clear that even Joshua wasn't there yet. He hadn't seen or heard Katie come home the previous night, so he was worried about her.

"Whatcha looking for?" Calvin asked, standing up and stretching.

"I'm looking for Katie," he answered.

"I think she's still in her room," his teammate told him. "I heard her come back in like the middle of the night, but she didn't stop and talk to anyone—just went straight into her room and closed the door."

"Huh," Damian mused. "That's not like her at all. And apparently Korbin let her go out on her own."

"No shit?" Calvin exclaimed. "It must have been a fluke."

"I hope so. I guess I'll go wake her up, make sure that she's okay."

Damian walked to her door and knocked as he looked down at his watch. It was six in the morning, and he could hear faint moans coming from inside. He pulled his hand back and stopped, thinking that maybe he'd heard wrong.

He leaned his head against the door and heard another moan come from within. Immediately his cheeks heated; he thought he might have interrupted some private time. He kept listening, though, and realized that the noise expressed more pain than pleasure.

He rattled the door knob, but it was locked. Panic flew through him as the sound became louder. He turned and slammed his shoulder into the door, rattling it almost loose. A groan slipped from his throat when he felt pain throb through him.

He shook his head and did it again, and this time the door flew open. He stumbled in and looked around the room, ready to kill a demon.

Instead Katie was laying on the bed fully clothed, although the top button of her jeans was open. She groaned again and grabbed her stomach, then rolled over onto her side.

"Katie!" Damian exclaimed, kneeling on the bed next to her. "Where does it hurt?"

She patted her stomach…gently.

"Does it hurt to press here?" he asked, pushing his fingers into her abdomen.

"No." She groaned louder, eyes closed.

"Do you have a fever?" he inquired, looking into her eyes. "Do you have allergies?"

"No," she responded.

She whispered something, but Damian couldn't hear her. He leaned closer and asked her to repeat herself, then held his breath, his head by her mouth.

"Too...*much*," she whispered.

"Too much what?" he asked.

"Too...much...*Italian*," she said, letting out a deep breath.

"Too much... Oh, God." Damian's laughter burst out like water breaking a dam. "You ate too much food."

"It's not funny!" she grumped, rolling on her back. "I have a food toddler in my belly right now."

"I just...I... Oh, God," he repeated, still laughing hysterically. "I thought something had gotten you. I seriously thought there was something wrong, but it was just food. Good *Lord*, it was just food."

Damian scooted to the end of the bed and rubbed his face, trying to calm his laughter. It was both funny and tragic at the same time.

He had thought... Well, he had thought a lot of things, but a full belly was not one them. When he had finally calmed himself enough he looked at the dresser, taking note of the two knives, short sword, and pistols lying there. If they were in her room, she had qualified to carry all of them.

"Damn! You shaped up pretty good, young lady," Damian told her, nodding toward the weapons. "I wasn't sure if you would ever get certified on them."

"It wasn't me." Katie nodded to him, but credited both him and the others. "I had good teachers."

"Good," he said, walking toward the door.

"Except for teaching me when to stop eating Italian," she said a little louder. "Then you guys are fucking *lousy*." She groaned pitifully.

Damian laughed, putting his hand in the air and waving as he walked out of the room. She needed to get the door fixed now.

On the south side of San Ysidro, a town within the San Diego County limits, things weren't so full of laughter and happiness.

The houses in the neighborhood were closely packed together, most of them mimicking the normal San Diego mission-style homes with their stucco sides and red tile roofs. They were old, the yards unkempt, and police sirens were a regular sound in the area. On this night a black Mercedes drove along the street , windows tinted so dark you couldn't see into the car. At the end of the block was a house that was just like the others on the outside, but on the inside a drug business flourished.

As the car pulled up in front, the silhouettes of the people scurrying about inside could be seen through the curtains. The driver parked and walked to the rear passenger door, standing in front of it and looking around before opening it. The politician got out of the car and pulled his jacket closed, buttoning it and looking around the neighborhood. He stepped forward and grimaced, picking his foot up and looking at the bottom—he had somehow managed to step in day-old vomit on the sidewalk. He scowled and held his handkerchief to his face as he scraped his shoe off in the grass.

"You're sure this is the place?" he asked, looking at the driver. The man nodded and started walking toward the front door.

The politician looked around with judgment on his face, then climbed the front steps and waited until the driver had opened the door for him. He nodded at the driver and stepped into the living room. There were several people completely fucked up on drugs lounging around along with the scurrying people, and two goons in front of him. They nodded for him to raise his arms so he did, allowing them to search his body for weapons or wires. When they were satisfied they looked at the driver, who stood at least a foot taller than either of them and was three times their width.

Suffice it to say, no one fucked with the driver at all that day. Instead, they stared up at him as he stood with his arms crossed over his chest and his eyes roving the room. He was not only the driver, but the bodyguard as well. The politician knew no one would fuck with him while his driver was near, no matter how badass they thought they were. The two men led the politician and his guard back to the end of the hallway, then stood aside and allowed the politician to enter.

"Hello, Alejandro," the politician said.

"The suit." He chuckled. *"El imbécil en el traje. El hombre de* T'Chezz."

"That's right," the politician said, walking to the front of Alejandro's desk. "The asshole in the suit. T'Chezz's man. You pegged me right."

"I could smell your demon before you got here," Alejandro said, his eyes burning red. "And you don't smell like you are too smart."

"Smart enough to stay out of T'Chezz's lair."

Alejandro laughed. "No you're not, suit. Please humor me with an explanation of why you have come to my house in broad daylight like this."

"I need your house." He looked around. "For summoning. This is directly from him."

"Why here?" Alejandro asked with a chuckle.

"I'll give you a cool twenty-five K to not ask questions."

The drug dealer shrugged and leaned back in his chair.

"Ain't no shit off my back."

"It's 'skin,'" the politician grumbled angrily.

"Whatever," Alejandro snarled. "Make it thirty, and we have a deal. I mean, I will have to empty everyone out of this joint, and possibly miss out on business. I mean, it was worth your time to come all the way out here, slumming it in your suit worth more than this whole place."

The politician clenched his fists and his teeth, trying to hold back his urge to rip the guy's throat out. He took a deep breath and cracked his neck to calm himself down, and slowly his patented smirk returned to his lips.

"All right, thirty thousand," he agreed, turning to his driver. "Retrieve the money for this *upstanding* drug dealer, would you please?

The driver looked at the drug dealer and narrowed his eyes. Alejandro chuckled, obviously not afraid of very much. The driver nodded to the politician and left the room.

"You know what, suit?" The drug dealer stood up and

walked around the desk. "Me and you—we ain't so different."

The drug dealer put his arm around the politician's shoulder and laughed as the politician pulled it off. He wiped his suit off and cleared his throat, pulling down on his jacket. He was not amused by the fact that he had to stand there and converse with someone so far below him.

"You see," Alejandro continued, walking back to his desk as he pointed between the two of them, "we both give people what they want. I'm just a bit more transparent about not giving a shit about their health. You... You try to put on a sly face, but I can read right through it."

At that moment the driver walked back into the house carrying a gym bag full of money, which he plopped down on the desk next to the dealer before walking over to the politician. The dealer opened it and whistled, then smiled as he pulled out a big stack of cash. He nodded his head and zipped the bag closed.

"Come on, boys." He waved to his two heavies, then looked at the politician. "How about the people in the living room? You want me to get them out of here?"

"No," the politician said, wiping off his hands on his handkerchief and giving the dealer a fake smile. "I suppose it will help to have them here."

"I should have asked for thirty-five," Alejandro grumbled as he walked out of the house. "I'm going to lose some seriously loyal customers on this damn deal."

The politician rolled his eyes as the dealer slammed the door behind him.

The politician carefully removed his jacket and hung it over a nearby chair, rubbing his hands together and closing his eyes as he settled himself and his demon. Then, with no expression on his face, he turned and stared at the driver, who was standing there with a couple of helpers who had shown up shortly after he walked back in with the gym bag.

"I need you to drag a few of those drugged-out addicts in here and drop them in the center of the floor." He waved a finger toward the center. "I'll move the furniture out while you start bringing them over."

The driver nodded and pushed his helpers, moving them toward the unconscious bodies lying around the house. The politician rolled his sleeves up and moved the furniture back against the walls, then stood back and watched until his men were done.

The helpers moved to the background with fear in their eyes as the politician pulled a small vial of blue dust from his pocket. Slowly he walked a circle clockwise around the bodies, pouring the dust on the floor. When he was done he turned and raised his arms over his head, his palms out and open.

"*Nos hie vocare te magnanime daemonium septuaginta duo. Exite nostrae tenebras paravimus corporis tui. Quod petis hic damnatio suscipiendum hoc tecum sumus,*" the politician chanted over and over. Each time he spoke, his voice was a little louder.

After the third time the house began to rattle loudly, and, in the circle, a massive monster started to materialize.

His curled-up body hovered over the floor.

The politician said the incantation for a final time, and this time the body of the beast unfurled in front of him. His jaws were clamped together and he snarled as his feet floated downward. The beast slowly lifted his head and turned toward the politician.

"T'Chezz's *vessel*," the beast whispered as he looked at his hands. "So he wasn't tricking me after all."

The politician shook his head. "No. He's not really a game player."

"Why the circle?" the demon asked, looking around him.

"Do you see the rope I placed through the circle?" the politician asked.

"Yes," the beast growled.

"I am going to light it on fire in just a moment, and no more than five minutes from that time it will break the circle. You will be free to do what you want. I've provided food and entertainment."

The beast followed the politician's gaze to the bodies beside him. He poked one of them; the human was still alive. He smiled and looked at the politician, nodding. The politician nodded slightly in return and stepped forward to pick up the end of the rope, lighting it on fire. Slowly it burned toward the circle, and the demon looked around in amazement.

"This is where we leave you." He dropped the flaming rope. "You know what your mission is, so I don't need to remind you."

The demon nodded. The politician looked at his driver and the help, nodding at them as well.

The men left the house and closed the door behind them, no longer interested in what happened next. They had done their jobs. The driver hurried forward and opened the door for the politician, who quickly climbed in.

No one wanted to be near that place when the demon broke free. The driver shut the door and hurried around to the other side, jumping in the driver's seat and taking off.

The politician looked over his shoulder at the shimmering light coming from the structure and then turned back, smiling.

He had completed his mission, and now it was up to T'Chezz to get things going. To take the next step toward his goals.

The black car turned the corner and accelerated out of sight, putting distance between it and the drug house. From within came the screams of the drug addicts locked inside with the monster. He had ingested his food and now sat in his circle, biting down on the neck of a screaming woman and ripping at her flesh until the noise had diminished and her body was limp.

He tossed the body to the side and stood up, then stepped carefully out of the circle. The spell had worked, and he was free to start his next round of terror.

He hadn't come to Earth to chew on drug addicts' necks.

No, he had come there for a reason—and he wouldn't be dealing with people who would just stand by and watch him make his move.

He walked toward the front door and grabbed the handle, casually ripping the door from its hinges.

He was free at last, *and no one was going to take that away.*

5

"There aren't any reports of the most recent incidents." Korbin tossed some papers aside. "For all intents and purposes, these articles say what the DEA told the reporters, word for word. There isn't anything here that gives us new information."

"There has to be something out there." Calvin tapped his leg, frustrated. "Even if it comes from that conspiracy theory paper's reporter who is always at the scene, asking us questions."

"Yeah," Korbin said, pointing at Calvin. "That's true. There is one particular woman, but I can't think of her name."

"Charlotte," Calvin answered. "Charlotte Guthrie."

Korbin raised an eyebrow. "Should I wonder why you know that name so well?"

"Nope." Calvin shrugged. "Just remembered it, that's all."

"Who else has met this girl?" Korbin asked.

"Katie, Garrett, Damian… Pretty much everyone."

Korbin reached over and called for Katie over the loud-speaker. If anyone could help him at that moment, it was probably her. They sat there quietly going over the articles in front of them until she showed up.

"Hey, boss," she said, sweaty from training and eyeing them both. "What can I do for you?"

Korbin greeted Katie with, "By the way, that cannoli you brought back was great! Almost as good as my grandma used to make." He derived considerable enjoyment from watching her turn slightly green at the mention of food, since Damian had told him the tale of her previous evening's overindulgence and its aftermath.

Katie smiled tentatively. "Am I in trouble?"

"No, not in trouble," Korbin replied. "I have a mission for you. You and Calvin are going to San Diego. I want you to check out Charlotte Guthrie, who works for an underground publication called *The Seeing Eye*. She approached you when we were taking you out of the old parking garage the night you were infected. I want you and Calvin to read up on any stories she has done about the Damned and go from there."

"And by go from there you mean…" Calvin looked at Korbin.

"I want you to connect with her. Get her alone and find out what she knows, if anything," Korbin explained. "I want you to *really* talk to her, if you know what I mean."

"Isn't that dangerous?" Katie looked between the two men. "Delving into that kind of reporting? I mean, that publication… They don't have the best credentials, and half their shit is made-up, like the woman who saw Jesus in her toast and then preached that her toaster was possessed by the devil."

"Hey, maybe it was. I've seen crazier." Calvin chuckled.

Katie was quiet for a moment. "True."

Pandora spoke up. *There is no fucking way we would possess a small electrical appliance. What a load of horseshit.*

"The thing is, she has intel—or at least she may," Korbin told them. "And if we have to dance with the devil... Wait."

Calvin's and Katie's faces curled into grimaces and Korbin shook his head, annoyed. "That was not what I meant," he admitted. "For obvious reasons, that was a very bad metaphor."

Pandora cackled. *Ask him if he knows the tango. I got those moves like Jagger.*

"Hey, if we have to dance with the devil to kick his ass, I'll learn the damn two-step," Katie assured them.

That was NOT what I said! Pandora huffed. *It's like you're ignoring me here.*

"The two-step, really?" Calvin laughed. "I mean, if the devil was dancing, it'd be more like the damn Tootsee Roll."

Really? As a black man, you are seriously killing your street cred.

"I could never do that." Katie shook her head.

"You're white." Calvin patted her on the shoulder. "It's all right. We won't judge you for that."

I do. I don't care what color you are! I will absolutely judge you for that shit.

"Gee, thanks." Katie smirked. "I was starting to think that I was destined to be second-best because I couldn't actually dance with the devil."

I'm right here. No need to go all dancing with the devil when you got me. Are you even fucking listening?

"Anyway." Korbin sighed. "Just try not to divulge too much information to her. We don't need a story coming out next week with everything you two lunatics told her because you got off-topic."

"Right," Katie agreed, clearing her throat and sitting up straight. "We will be *on*-topic and careful the entire time."

"And for God's sake, don't let her get killed," Korbin warned.

Katie pursed her lips. "In all fairness, we never actually *try* to get anyone killed. That would be pretty fucked up of us."

I do try to get people killed, or at least I did. It's been a bit anemic lately.

Are you done? Katie asked. *I mean, some of that was halfway funny, but I'm in a serious conversation here.*

You keep talking to me like I'm not wanted at the adult conversation table, and I'll give you a serious case of heartburn... heavy on the burn.

Duly noted, and I can't always carry on a three-way—

Pandora snickered.

CONVERSATION! Katie sighed. *Geez, it's like I can't say anything without you going right to the gutter.*

You wouldn't question that if you just enjoyed ONE NIGHT in the gutter with me.

I'm pretty sure I can do without that.

I could draw you a picture.

How about I get some crayons for you?

Did you just diss me? I think you did! If I fucking knew what crayons were, I'd make you shoot flames out your ass next time you fart.

Lalalalala... I'm going back to the conversation, and don't you fucking dare!

Hahahahahaha! Now I know what you fear, Katie Maddison!

"Yeah, boss, we aren't *trying* to kill folks." Calvin echoed, fucking with Korbin.

"The reporter has lasted this long on the fringes. I'd hate for us to be the ones who got her burned by the fire." Korbin shrugged. "The girl is just trying to make a living in her profession."

"And what profession would that be?" Calvin replied.

"Journalism," Korbin gruffed, standing up from the table. "Human being. That's all you need to know. She's a human being, and deserves to be protected."

"We got it, sir." Katie laughed. "Just giving you a hard time."

Korbin's eyes narrowed, but there was a glint of amusement in them. "Your cover: you are a very rich couple who have come to town for business."

"Oh, Lord." Katie looked at Calvin. "Don't think for two seconds that you are getting any."

"What?" Calvin asked, surprised. "I was thinking about what not to tell this journalist, not what sex I won't be getting as a fake husband—not that as a husband I would be thinking of getting any sex."

"Mmmhmm," Katie said, standing up. "All right, *husband*, let's get this show on the road."

"Okay, I know this is for show and all, but there is no need to throw around the H-word." Calvin's voice was a bit on the pleading side. "You could really end up jinxing me."

"Come on." Katie sighed and walked out of the room.

"Those two will drive me to drink," Korbin murmured. They continued to argue as they went down the hall, then down to the garage. He looked at what was on his desk that had to be finished.

"I think something else is in order. *Anything* else." Korbin stood up and left the office to walk over to the other building.

Perhaps he would take a look around and go over the books. As he walked up he saw a tall, beautiful woman who was about his age standing out front and looking at him.

"Hello," Korbin said.

"Oh, hello, Mr. Korbin," she replied with a roll of the "r." "We haven't formally met." She held out a hand, which he took and shook. "I am Mamacita. I own the house that Joshua is staying in."

"Oh, right." He smiled. "How is he doing?"

"Good! I just came to help him out a bit, thank him for his generosity at our home." She smiled. "Running a business can be difficult; stressful, even. It's all about pacing yourself and thinking through decisions." She turned around to look at the building. "At least, that's what I keep telling him."

"Well, I appreciate that." He nodded slightly. "It's very good advice. I'm going to head into the office for a bit. Don't mind me."

Korbin smiled and walked away, realizing that Mamacita had a fairly good head on her shoulders.

When he made it into the office, he stuck that thought in the back of his mind and started digging through the purchases. About halfway through, he called Joshua over to join him in the office so he could ask for specifics about the different costs he found in the books for the metals.

"They are what I negotiate," Joshua said.

Korbin ran a hand through his hair. "I get that, but for someone who isn't used to business, it can be overwhelming. Anyone could miss something," Korbin said with a smile. "Mamacita?" he called.

"Yes?" she yelled back.

"Would you come in here for a moment?"

"Sure," she said, rounding the corner. "What can I do for you?"

"Here is the information for two different metal companies," Korbin said, jotting down some numbers. "I want you to call them and order the metals in the amounts we need on this page."

"Okay," she said, eyeing Korbin.

Mamacita took the phone Korbin offered and dialed the first number, and as soon as she got the sales rep on the phone she started to negotiate the price.

Joshua watched her in awe, almost shocked to see anyone speak with her intensity.

She had a way with words; it was like she was made for a job like that. By the time she was done, she had managed to secure the materials for a quarter of the price Joshua had been paying.

"Holy shit," he said, shaking his head. "That was crazy, like you saved so much money right then." He paused, his voice dropping a bit. "I don't know if I could ever do something like that. Those people know how to push my buttons," he admitted.

"Because you *let* them, *mijo*." Mamacita smiled.

"Good job," Korbin replied, clapping his hands to get Joshua's attention. When he had it, he pointed to Mamacita. "And *that* is how you do business."

Korbin closed the book and tossed the cabinet's keys to Mamacita. He glanced at Joshua, who was still completely shocked by what had just happened. Korbin couldn't help but chuckle to himself as he walked around the desk and put his hand on Mamacita's shoulder.

"You're hired," he told her, looking straight ahead.

"What?" she squawked as he smiled and walked out the door.

"Hired?" She looked at Joshua, who was pondering the whole episode. "Like I wanted a job? Who does he think he is, just waltzing in here and pointing fingers at people? Bossing them around?"

She huffed and puffed, standing there with her hands on her hips as Korbin walked across the manufacturing floor.

"*I am a strong and independent woman!*" she yelled. "I do what I want, when I want to do it. I do not take orders from any man!"

Korbin opened the front door and walked out, not even looking back at her. She watched as the door shut behind him, blocking the sunlight.

She stood there for a moment longer, and a smile began to move over her lips. She had always made her own choices in her life, but there was something about this job that she couldn't resist—or maybe it was the man behind it.

"So," she said quietly to herself. "Mr. Big, Tall, and Hunky thinks he can just come in here, hire me, and walk out." She bit her lower lip. "Well, I think I will just go right ahead and get a bit of my own back."

She straightened her arms and spun around to stare at Joshua, who was starting to recover from his amazement. She chuckled, loving how innocent that kid was, and how he was going to get the attention he needed.

She adjusted her expression and put on a hard face.

"Come here," she snapped. "Pull up a chair next to mine. We are going to go through every single one of your purchases since this company started, and don't leave anything out. If you want the company to succeed, you have to learn from your mistakes and your successes. That is how great people become *greater*, Joshua—they observe, and they figure out from the best how to make the system even better. Eventually you will be able to make these choices with your eyes closed. You won't need Mamacita here looking over your shoulder every step of the way."

"Yes, ma'am," Joshua said meekly, hurrying across the room to grab a chair and pushing it back in front of him. "I'm ready to learn."

"I'll give *him* 'you're hired.'"

"You wouldn't be so upset if you had just slept with that guy from the cabana," Elizabeth commented to her friend. "Now you are upset because the vacation is over, and we are stuck at the San Diego airport waiting for our flight back home."

"It's not about him," Sarah told her, "and there are a lot worse places we could be stuck than at an airport. Take this opportunity, for example." She pointed out the window.

"What?" Elizabeth asked, walking up to the glass and watching a sleek black jet roll down the runway and pull to the side for unloading.

"Where else would you see a private jet stop all the traffic?" She laughed. "And they are unloading right there. We get to see someone famous."

The girls stood in the window staring at the Killers' private jet. As the door opened they moved closer, basically pressing their faces against the glass.

The stairs lowered to the ground and a female emerged, dressed in a calf-length tight black dress, suit jacket, and black heels. Her hair was pulled back tightly, and her large-lensed sunglasses hid most of her face.

Directly behind her was a very handsome, very sharply-dressed black man. His hair was freshly cut, his suit was pressed perfectly, and his glasses hid *his* eyes as well.

As they got off the plane they looked around for a moment, then got directly into a blacked-out SUV. The guy was the driver, and the woman climbed into the passenger seat and shut the door. As soon as they drove off, the girls turned to one another.

"See?" Sarah told her. "Only in California. It's not all bad."

"That *is* kinda cool," Elizabeth agreed, then her eyes narrowed and she asked, "Which of the Kardashians was that?"

6

"**O**kay," Katie demanded, taking her glasses off. "Where are we going first?"

"First we are going to this tavern in South Park, or near it, called Hamilton's," Calvin told her as he took a right turn.

"Why?" Katie asked.

"Because...*beer*." He chuckled. "And food."

"I guess that's a good enough reason." She shrugged.

They drove up the highway, and after exiting took several different streets. Katie had to admit she was very glad she wasn't the one driving, since California drivers terrified the shit out of her. She was used to Las Vegas driving, which was mostly slow and steady due to the freakishly wide multi-lane roads all over the place. Las Vegas had a bunch of cheap land and they weren't afraid to use it.

When they finally got to the bar, she was relieved to be done with roads for a little while.

The two of them went inside and looked around. The bar was a hole in the wall, but it was charming in some ways. Over the bar there were hundreds of beer tap handles.

On the wall above the active taps was a giant chalk-board, with the names of the available beers hand-printed in different colored chalks across it. The selection was unbelievable. There were beers from all over the world on their draft list, and if you wanted a bottle, there were a ton of them as well, all stacked neatly in the fridge against the wall.

Katie took a seat at the bar and pulled a menu from the stack. She was starving, since they'd left Las Vegas in such a hurry. It was good to feel hungry again—this was the first time since she'd allowed Pandora to talk her into gorging herself at the Italian restaurant.

There had come a point where she couldn't speed up the digestion and elimination process any further, so she'd just had to wait it out. That kind of food orgy could not and would not happen again.

Quite so soon.

So instead of a repeat, she decided that having a salad would be the best course of action.

"This place is nuts." Calvin grinned, looking around.

Katie narrowed her eyes. "I thought you had been here before?"

"Nah. I read about it on the plane, so I figured we would give it a try," he told her. "I didn't want to rush right into a crowded restaurant in downtown San Diego. All the reviews said that despite being a hole in the wall, the place was really good. It's not often I get such a choice selection of brews." He snickered. "The guys back at the base are going to be so jealous of this."

"Yes, they will be…and Korbin will be pissed," she joked.

Calvin agreed. "You're right. Better not show them until we get back."

"It's better to ask permission than forgiveness?" Katie said, tilting her head.

"That, but backward," Calvin replied.

Katie thought about it a second, "Well, damn. I *did* say it wrong."

"Besides, if I'm going to get demon guts all over me, I need to be properly lubricated beforehand."

"Hey, you two." The bartender lightly wiped the bar down as he walked over to them. "What can I get for you?"

"I will have the…" Calvin looked up at the sign. "I'll have the Beachwood Red Ale."

The bartender smiled at Katie. "And you?"

"Do you have hot tea?" she asked.

"We normally do, but we are all out," he explained. "We do have the Lipton raspberry."

Katie nodded, not sure she could refuse at that point. He walked back with Calvin's beer and Katie's prepackaged iced tea.

She was more than a little pissed at the fact that she was going to have to drink it.

Kill horrible demons, check.

Fight for her right to have a brewed cup of tea? Uncheck.

What the hell was up with her unwillingness to push back on the small things? She should have just told him to bring her a beer.

The two of them ordered some food, and found a small table in the back corner to sit down at. Katie almost felt claustrophobic even with the bar mostly empty, and couldn't imagine what it would be like if it were packed like the bars got in Vegas.

Everyone would be a big pile of sweat and drunkenness, baking in the San Diego sunshine. It would be absolutely miserable.

"So, do you think this reporter will have real information about what is going on?" Calvin asked.

"I don't know." Katie shrugged. "I'm inclined to say no, but honestly, there is a chance that she does. I mean, she shows up at most of the killings and I have no idea how she tracks us or finds us. There is a really good chance that if she does that to us, she has a handle on who the other guys are too."

"Maybe." Calvin sounded unconvinced.

"Of course, she could have absolutely nothing except news on the next talking banana," Katie continued. "In that case, we will just be fueling her fire. If she doesn't know anything and we yanked her off the street, she's gonna know something big is going on."

"I know." Calvin sighed. "But we have to do it, since Korbin wants it to be done. And we have to make sure we protect her like we promised to. Until then, though," he lifted his bottle, "I am going to drink this beer...and probably get another."

The middle of the night was a normal time for people in

San Ysidro neighborhoods to be lurking in the streets, especially in that neighborhood.

The drug house had been quiet for hours and no one had come to check on it, neither for the fire in the living room nor the screaming and crying when the demon had made the people dropped into his circle his first meal.

The guy walking toward the house now was nothing more than a junkie looking for his next fix from his normal drug dealer, with whom he shopped every time he had enough cash.

He scratched the side of his face and yawned as he walked up the steps to the front door. He was used to seeing some serious muscle out there at that time of night, but figured they were having a party inside or something.

He knocked on the door and stood there rubbing his hands together, looking around in paranoia. After a couple of minutes he knocked again, surprised that no one had answered the door. Alejandro had always been open twenty-four hours a day, seven days a week.

The druggie shrugged his shoulders and opened the unlocked door slowly and walked inside.

"Hey, Alejandro," he called, his burnt-out coke nose twitching. "I'm here for… whoa!"

He tripped over something and landed on the floor on all fours, cursing. He stared at the red puddle underneath him and slowly he lifted his hands in disgust, watching the blood drip down them.

Then he focused on the room, where there were the pieces of bodies strewn all over the floor. He swallowed hard. He wanted to scream, but nothing would come out.

After scrambling to his feet he looked at the rug to the side, which had a large burn mark in the center.

There were bodies fucking everywhere, and the stench of blood permeated the place. He had been half out of his mind to begin with, but this sent him over the edge.

He scrambled to the door and ran as fast as he could toward the front yard.

He stumbled down the steps—fell off them, really—and rolled across the lawn, his breathing so heavy he damn near passed out. If there was a way to sober someone up?

He had walked right into it.

Three blocks down the street two cops were parked on the edge of the neighborhood, taking it easy while watching the streets like they normally did at that hour.

They were used to seeing crazy shit going on with the junkies and the homeless in the area, so at first they didn't even notice the guy, who was covered in blood, trying to run a straight line down the street toward them.

"So yeah, the sergeant was right there with the girl," Stone told his partner Holden. "He gave zero shits that everyone was staring at him and the woman, and one half his age, too. I bet he thought he could get away with it. Well, then his wife shows up and just about kills him right there in the middle of the bar."

"No fucking way," Holden complained, shaking his head. "I always miss the good shit."

Stone cracked up at that. "How is daddy life treating you now?"

"It's good, most days." Holden chuckled. "It's tough when I get off the night shift because the baby's up and the wife's up. They try not to bother me, but we live in a shoe-box-sized house and we are unable to really do anything quietly with the baby."

"Yeah, but you've been saving up for a new house, right?" Stone asked.

Holden nodded and frowned. "Yeah, but it all depends on whether I make rank this time around," he told Stone. "I need to make more money to be approved for the house we want. That, or we are going to have to move away from this town or even state. It's so fucking expensive here; we can't do anything."

"I feel you, dude," Stone commiserated. "My girlfriend wants the whole nine: the house, the dog, the kids, and the picket fence. It's not her making me question getting all of that, it's the fucking price of living here in Cali."

"We could go be cops in Mayberry," Holden suggested with a twinkle in his eye.

That cracked Stone up completely. "Yeah, right. I would go nuts." He shook his head, "No fucking way."

"What the hell?" Holden exclaimed, squinting into the gloom.

"What?" Stone asked quickly, following his partner's line of sight until he found what Holden was watching.

They watched the druggie run down the street, his hands covered in something red and his face pale as a ghost. It looked like he might just have shit his pants.

The druggie spotted the car and the cops both got out, figuring he was headed in that direction anyway. As he got closer, the officers put their hands on their guns.

"That's far enough," Holden commanded, raising his hand.

"What's all over you?" Stone challenged.

The guy was completely incoherent, talking so fast and shaking so badly that they couldn't understand a word he was saying.

Holden attempted to calm the distraught man. "Take a deep breath. Speak slowly and clearly so we can understand you."

The man's eyes bulged, and his words continued to be lost in frightened sobs and gulps for air.

"Breathe, man," the officer repeated, his patience wearing thin.

The man continued to gibber, waving his arms in the direction he'd run from. He was clearly high, and both officers could see the blood coating him.

"STOP!" Holden finally called, raising his sidearm but not pointing it directly at the man...

Yet.

"Now take a motherfucking deep breath or I am going to drop you right here on this street!"

"Okay, okay." The junkie cringed, raising one hand and putting the other on his knee. "Just give me one second. Look, I know you think I'm a junkie, right? Well, I don't want the motherfucking drugs anymore." He pointed back the way he had come. "I just found a bunch of dead bodies and what looks like some serious fucking voodoo devil shit in that house down there at the end of the block."

Stone sneered. "Are you sure you're not high as a kite?"

"No," he denied angrily. "How else would I have all this blood on me?"

"All right," Holden allowed, with a doubtful glance at Stone. "Take us to the house so we can see this for ourselves."

"Okay, follow me." The druggie turned back toward the house, and hurried up the sidewalk with the officers following closely behind him.

"You know shit's bad when a junkie is leading the police to the house he buys his shit from," Stone remarked dryly. "Like, this might be one of the first signs of the apocalypse."

"Right," Holden agreed with a low chuckle. "What's next? Bank robbers returning the cash?"

The guys kept up the snarky banter all the way to the house.

Holden looked left and right before shining the flashlight into the open doorway. Something sparkled in the dark and Holden stepped closer, pulling his brows together.

"What the hell is that?" he wondered aloud, stepping toward the house.

The two officers shone their flashlights through the door from the porch, and the beams showed them several different body parts.

"That's... That's a *head*!" Stone put his hand to his face and groaned, wanting to puke right then and there.

Immediately Holden reached for his gun and spun around to point it at the junkie. "Put your hands up," he bellowed. "Put them up over your head."

"Officer, I didn't do nothing," the druggie begged. "I swear I found them like this."

"Then who did this?" Holden demanded, pushing the man down on all fours.

The druggie began to weep. "As far as I know, the only one that can be at fault is the devil himself," he cried, trembling in fear.

Back in Vegas, things were a lot more relaxed and quiet. Mamacita had gone back to her home with the girls for the evening. She sat down at her computer and thought for a moment, trying to decide the best search terms for what she was interested in buying.

It had been many years since she had needed appropriate clothing for work. So long, in fact, that she didn't exactly know what size she was in the brands she found.

Still, she needed something professional to wear into the office now that she was going to be doing the ordering and pretty much all the administrative work.

"What clothes are you ordering?" Lily, one of the girls from the brothel, asked. "Are you getting back into the business with us?"

"No." Mamacita chuckled and gave her a coy smile and a wink. "I'm buying *business* clothes."

"What's the difference?" Lily asked innocently. "We work for a business, right?"

"Yes, but these clothes are for working while you are vertical," Mamacita explained. "It's another type of game men and women play—one where we let the men believe they are in the driver's seat, when really we tell them where to go."

"Oh?" Lily inquired, with a look that said she didn't really understand.

"Don't worry about it, sweetie. You just keep doing what you know." Mamacita smiled. "I've got a new challenge."

The girl walked away nodding happily and Mamacita

leaned forward, staring at the black dress suit on the Versace website.

It was nice, but not at all what she was looking for. She was intending to buy herself horizontal outfits, and she was pretty sure she had a crush on one specific man.

She knew it was her turn to have a good time, to show how intelligent she was, and to be the star of her own life for once. She just wished she knew exactly what they did for a living. Running a business where she didn't know what the product was might be a bit of a challenge, but she liked those, and she certainly wasn't going to pass the opportunity by.

Maybe she would find out something she didn't want to know, or maybe she would find out something that she had known all along. Either way she was going shopping, and she was going to make sure she looked damn good at work.

No matter *what* he was into.

Mamacita sat back in the chair, thinking about the weapons, their obvious fitness, and the grit in their eyes. It took her back.

Back to a time before she had become what she was today.

Was it time to accept her past? Her lips pressed together as she continued to review the clothes and make notes of where she might want to shop in town.

The past was perhaps better left there.

7

There were at least three squad cars parked on the San Ysidro street. Everyone was talking—or in some cases yelling—trying to figure out what the hell happened in that drug house and where the remainder of the bodies had gone.

The parts they had found told them nothing.

No way the evidence was eaten. Nothing just *ate* body parts.

A black SUV pulled up in front of the house and parked, and after a moment an attractive woman and a very handsome man climbed out and looked around like there was nothing surprising happening.

"Stop right there," one of the cops ordered, putting up his hand. "I don't know who the hell you think you are, but this is a crime scene. I don't care how much money you have—you can't just come in here when something like this is going on."

"We are your backup," Calvin replied with a smirk. "Actually, you and your partner are now *our* backup."

The cop did a double-take. "What?"

"Let me guess," Katie cut in with a wave toward the house. "Dead bodies or parts of dead bodies all over the house, a circle on the ground, possibly a small fire? Am I getting warm?"

"Oh, *shiiit*..." The cop's eyes widened and he took a half-step back. "I thought it was just a rumor. One of those stupid things that gets blown out of proportion."

"What?" Katie asked.

"You're the D squad," he replied, glancing back and forth between Calvin and Katie.

"The *what*?" Calvin asked

"The D squad," the cop repeated, pointing to the two of them. "The demon squad. We thought it was an old wives' tale or just something our boss told us to scare the hell out of us, but when we got here today it was obvious." He jerked a thumb toward the house. "I'm guessing this was no human killer. And now that *you* guys are here, I'm willing to bet that guess is almost a definite."

"I wouldn't say it was definite just yet." Katie walked toward the house.

"Are you fucking kidding me?" a second cop interrupted in disbelief. "You are going to believe little Miss Priss in her six-inch heels and the guy in the designer suit who come waltzing up here like they are in a movie of some sort? You are the most gullible asshole I have ever met."

Katie made a moue and walked toward the second cop. "You are so cynical," she told him. "I know it's *really* hard to believe that there is someone even more badass than you."

Katie put her finger on his cheek and trailed it down his face, and he stared at her for a moment, unable to say a word. Calvin looked at him and shook his head, somewhat surprised by how entranced these guys were by Katie.

"The big bad demon guy came in and ruined your evening?" Katie pouted. She tapped the cop's face, snapping him out of his daze. "Well, just a note for you and your friends...*we like to be called The Damned.*"

Katie's eyes flashed bright red and she let out a gleeful cackle, then walked into the house.

Calvin snorted, thoroughly entertained by just how fast the guy's face changed given one little sneak peek at the demon inside her.

Nothing beat showing the truth to a non-believer, then sitting back and watching the chaos that ensued.

Calvin patted the cop on the back and walked past him into the house, and he was still smiling when he entered. He was amused—royally amused—and he wanted to see the mischief on Katie's face as well. However, when he reached her he saw no mischief or humor in her expression, only sadness and anger.

Calvin stopped and took stock of the room around him. He had been so ready to see carnage that when he did, his mind had passed right over it.

"Holy shit," Calvin breathed, looking around at the scene.

"I know," Katie agreed wholeheartedly.

"Hey, how did you do that thing?" Calvin waggled a finger in front of his eyes to demonstrate. "You know, the thing where your eyes flashed red? We have the ring around them, but I never thought we could actually make them red like that."

Katie shrugged. "I don't know. I saw Korbin do it. It's more of a control thing; like a party trick in some ways, I suppose."

"Well, I need to work on that. It's nuts, and it freaks the hell out of people." There was a hint of admiration in Calvin's voice as he spoke the words.

Katie grimaced. "I'd really rather not freak people out. If we do, they might think we do stuff like," she swept an upturned palm around to indicate the gore coating the room, "this disgusting carnage for no good reason besides boredom."

Calvin clenched his right hand. "What freaks me out about all of it is the fact that those demons, or some like them, are inside of us," he growled. "That means that *every one* of us has it in them to do this. Every damn one of us has a brutal and disgusting killer inside."

He scuffed his boot miserably on the one clean patch of floor. "You would think that because of that, we wouldn't be trusted no matter who we work for," he finished quietly.

"I don't think we *are* trusted," Katie said, patting Calvin's shoulder in sympathy as she looked him in the eyes. "I think that, no matter what happens in this world, we will always be feared. No one will ever fully trust us." She shrugged. "But in the end, is that such a terrible thing? Is it wrong for them to fear people with demons so strong it affects the way they fight? Is it wrong to be scared that something will go wrong with our demons? That we too will end up creating a horror like this?"

Katie stepped delicately over the fast-congealing puddle of blood, shaking her head as she answered her own question. "Nope, it's not wrong at all."

"How does it look?" Korbin asked, pacing back and forth behind Derek.

"It's getting there," Derek grumped, typing something into the computer.

"How did you get into this stuff?" Korbin asked, pausing to squint at the screen over Derek's shoulder.

Derek kept typing as he glanced up. "Honestly, I took some courses in college and then taught myself more," he explained with a small, satisfied smile. "It fascinated me, and I've always related to numbers. They just come to me, like another language I understand it without really learning it. I don't know…I guess maybe this was my true calling."

Korbin clapped him on the shoulder. "Well, you are using it in *this* world, and that is incredibly important."

"Okay," Derek said, turning around to face him. "Tell me again exactly what you are looking for."

Korbin straightened and became serious again. "I am looking for a program of spiders; ones that can crawl over the internet, pulling data about paranormal comments from social media," he told Derek. "I need to open up new avenues for tips; ways we can find these demons before they massacre hundreds of people again. I know it's really 'Big Brother' of me, but I only want the paranormal activity. Is that even possible?"

"Anything is possible," Derek assured him. "So basically, you want to be able to scan the system to find every conversation that seems demonic in nature and send it to us so we can decide if we need to act on it?"

"Yep, exactly," Korbin confirmed. "But it is really important that the people who can use it are very restricted. I mean *very* restricted. The fewer people who have the ability to use this, the less likely it is to be abused."

"Right." Derek nodded. "Well, I would restrict access to just me and you at first."

Korbin grinned. "That's smart. So, you can do it?"

"Yeah, no problem." Derek resumed typing as he spoke. "You have to use some sort of social database service. It allows for faster development, but it will increase the monthly bills."

Korbin raised an eyebrow. "How much higher?"

"Noticeably higher," Derek replied hesitantly.

Korbin sighed. "Okay, if you do it, can you set it up to be billed directly to me?"

"Yeah, sure," Derek confirmed. "That's no problem."

Korbin beamed and patted him on the back. "All right, do it, then."

Korbin left the room and walked down the hallway toward the main area. He was getting everything into place —everything he would need to be more up to speed on the whereabouts of these demons, what they were planning, and possibly how to stop an attack before it took place. He had never thought of using technology as an ally in the fight against *this* terrorist, but it was turning out to be one of his greatest resources.

The only problem with all of it was the fact that *he* had

no idea how to use it, couldn't read it, didn't want to learn about it, and didn't know if he could rely on it. It was something that the others were not aware of, though, and he liked it like that.

There were aspects of the job he had that meant he had to keep secrets even from the people who were closest to him. He wanted badly to be a part of the team like everyone else, but there was a level of secrecy that he had to keep that the others didn't.

He felt like he could never fully be part of the team. He always had to conceal the truth of himself and hold the curtain closed to hide the lies that were going on behind the scenes.

It was exhausting, but it was *necessary*.

Katie and Calvin combed through the tattered limbs strewn around the room, unable to miss that they had been torn from the bodies rather than removed with any kind of weapon. It was obvious that the killer had utilized these people for lunch and nothing more.

Calvin walked into the back room and stared at the desk in the corner where the drug dealer would have sat. That was where the demon would have made a deal with him to be released from his chains and join them on Earth.

Katie walked into the back room, wrinkling her nose as she spoke. "This demon is strong. I'm just confused about what happened here."

"Yeah, me too," Calvin concurred. "There is that circle with the rope on it, but what about the human to be used as a capsule? Who did the ceremony? Who brought the demon up from hell?"

"I don't know," Katie mused. "But whoever it was, they had to have a pretty powerful demon themselves. They didn't stay long if they did it. They knew what they were bringing back. I can smell mojan dust. It was used to enclose the circle and keep the beast inside, but why use it if your whole purpose is to let it loose on the public?"

"Fear," Calvin stated flatly. "Whoever it was knew what this guy or demon could do, and he feared that."

Katie chewed her lip. "Yes. He made a failsafe, something that would give him time to get out before the demon did."

"That means the beast started out in the circle and knew already what to do to get out and to go out into society." Calvin looked around nervously. "That means he is an old demon, someone who knows our kind very well. Someone who didn't need a guide, just someone to push the buttons on this end to get him in."

"Someone with a very big shoe," Katie replied, looking down in front of her.

"That's a damn big footprint for a human." Calvin's eyes widened as he examined the print.

"That is *not* a human print," Katie pointed out, "unless our human is bigger than Shaq."

Calvin narrowed his eyes. "I don't get it. We thought that demons could only be in their hosts. I've never seen a host taken over that fast. Fast, but not *that* fast."

"Maybe we were wrong," Katie admitted. "Maybe the demons, or at least the stronger ones, *don't* need human bodies to survive."

"But yours is strong," Calvin argued.

Katie shook her head, dismissing Calvin's reasoning. "She didn't need my body. She was forced into it." She thought back to her drug-clouded possession night. "I saw her as plain as day in her own human-looking body that night."

Pandora snickered. *I'm damned good-looking, you must admit.*

I'm not admitting anything more to Calvin!

Calvin considered that for a moment. "Okay, but could a human capsule arrive through this process? One who had been sent to hell?"

"We are not our human bodies," Katie told him. "The bodies are just capsules, and when we die those capsules allow the soul to escape, to move on. There would be no human body in hell, just its soul."

Not always technically true, Pandora whispered.

Katie figured she would go down that rabbit hole another time

He looked around. "So, here we had a demon who scared the person conjuring it so much they were afraid to stay and help it enter the world, but still thought it was a good idea to do so. A full-fledged demon came through whatever portal was opened, fed, and then went into the city. Why have there been no reports about sightings yet? Why are people not completely freaking out about this?"

Katie enlightened him. "It hasn't shown itself yet. It is hiding and growing in strength by eating anyone that gets in its way, but it is lying low. Waiting."

Calvin made a face. "Waiting for what?"

Katie walked around the room, sensing the creatures

that had been there before. She ran her hand through the air over the circle.

She paused and looked at Calvin, meeting his eyes. "It's waiting for *us*."

"For *us*?" Calvin exclaimed, slipping his hand to the butt of his pistol. "Why us?"

"It knows we are hunting its kind," she told him. "It wants to grow an army to fight us."

Katie leaned down and picked up a small strand of hair. She held it up to the light. She wasn't sure who it belonged to, but it was just about the only clue that she had. For a creature that had just completely slaughtered so many, it was apparently incredibly hygienic.

"Not that hygienic," Pandora said, and sniffed the air using Katie's nose. *Oh, shit.*

"What?" Katie panicked. *"What is 'oh shit?'"*

"Open your senses, because this is about to get ugly," she said.

Katie straightened up and took a deep breath, her eyes darting to the front door. She could smell the demon, almost as if its scent were some sort of tracking device. She turned to Calvin with wide eyes.

"I can smell it," she exclaimed. "It's *close*."

She kicked off her heels and reached into her backpack, pulling out her normal calf-high black boots. She laced them tightly, making sure every single string was latched. When she was done she tightened her bag's straps, ensuring it was secure. She looked at Calvin with a growl and a grin. "You ready to kick some motherfucking demon ass?"

He matched her grin with one of his own. "Fuck yeah, I am!"

"Come on!" They darted toward the door, and Katie threw it open.

"Follow us in the cars," Calvin yelled as they sprinted past the two cops they had talked to before and down the block, twisting and turning through the streets.

The cops scrambled, dropping their coffees as they raced for their patrol car. When they got in they took off after Katie and Calvin, leaving the others at the house.

"These are some super-fast motherfucking human beings," Stone marveled.

"Yeah," Holden replied, shaking his head as Stone hit the brakes, squealed around a corner, and slammed the accelerator to the floor. "It's unnatural," he continued, "but it's part of the job, so step on it. Don't lose those fucking freaks."

8

Katie bolted down the alleyway faster than Calvin had seen anyone move before. He was fast, but not *that* fast.

Her boots glided over the surface of the street, barely touching the ground at all. She leapt and rebounded objects like they were trampolines placed there just for her.

Calvin couldn't keep up, but he needed to stay in contact with her, no matter what. It was vital that they not split up, but he couldn't hang.

"Katie," he called, slowing his pace.

She looked over her shoulder at him, stopping as he came up to her. "Are you all right?"

"I'm fine," Calvin huffed, breathing heavily. "I can't keep up with you, and neither can the cops. Look at them with their lights flashing, almost killing people trying to keep up with you. We need to catch the demon and I don't want you to slow down, but I need to be able to communicate with you. Turn on your earbud. I can triangulate the cops' system with that and your updates, so I can zero in on you. And every time you make a turn, yell it out. That way we can be right behind you."

"All right," Katie said reaching up and pressing the button on her earpiece. "It's on."

"Good, now go." Calvin waved her away. "But be *careful*. Don't be a fucking hero, Katie. Keep your space, but let this son of a bitch know you didn't come alone. That today it's just us, but tomorrow it will be an entire army. Protect your stomach and face just like we taught you, and ask your demon for a little bit of help."

No need to ask, Pandora growled.

"All right." Katie nodded. "I'll be okay. I always am, and I don't plan on dying today."

"Better fucking not." Calvin laughed, slapping hands with her.

As she bolted away, the wind from her departure blew old papers and trash around in the alleyway.

Calvin watched as she disappeared down the street and around a corner, smiling to himself. She was definitely a badass—no one could deny that. Calvin closed his eyes and centered on the sound of the cop car, which was quickly approaching. He turned to his right and started sprinting for the street. As he approached, he leapt through the air and landed on the hood of the patrol car.

"Get out," he growled to the cop in the passenger seat, his head hanging over the side. "I need your seat."

Holden nodded and threw himself in the back. Calvin slid inside and looked at the other cop, motioning with his hand for him to take off. He reached down and pulled the radio from its cradle into his lap, fiddling with the wires to try to get a signal out.

Meanwhile Katie ran after the demon's scent, jumping fences, leaping over moving cars, and climbing stairs on the outside of buildings like she was a fucking superhero. She looked around her as they headed out of the populated area toward an old six-story building. She could sense the demon more strongly than ever.

Slow down, Pandora whispered. *You are very close.*

Katie slowed, and came almost to a stop, then ducked behind a dumpster at the foot of the building. She peeked up, but couldn't see a thing. She looked around her, pressing on her ear piece.

"Calvin," she whispered. "Come in, Calvin. Can you hear me?"

There was a quiet crackle in her ear, then Calvin's voice.

"I got you," he confirmed. "Where are you?"

"I'm at the foot of a six-story building," she told him. "I ran straight, so it's maybe seven blocks from where you left me."

"We see it," he replied. "We are driving down the main boulevard."

"I have to go up there," Katie whispered. "He's on the roof."

"Can you get into the building?" Calvin asked.

"Maybe, but I don't like corners and hallways," she admitted, looking around for a solution. "Too risky, too dangerous. There is a ladder on the side of the building—a service ladder. It goes all the way up to the roof where this bastard is. I can smell his rotten skin all the way from the ground. He has gotten stronger since the house."

"All right, we are coming up on it," he came back. "Go to the ladder and start making your way up, but be careful."

"No shit, Sherlock." Katie chuckled. "You too."

"Nah." Calvin grinned in reply, and even though she couldn't see him she could hear it in his voice.

Katie crept slowly from her hiding space and toward the ladder. She didn't know where on the roof the creature was, but she knew she had to get there before he moved. The sun had come up during the chase, and it was about time for kids to head to school. She needed to keep him away from them.

When she reached the ladder she jumped upward and pulled herself up two rungs at a time. She couldn't afford to waste time. When she reached the place where the ladder met the roof she paused, breathing heavily and resting for just a moment. She didn't know what she would find up there, or if she could take it on her own. She just knew it was her duty to try, and she wasn't going to sit around and cry over it.

Pandora had her back. She didn't want Katie to die any more than she herself did, but that didn't mean they were invincible. Pandora might be a badass demon, but that didn't mean she'd *never* lost a fight. For her it would be no big deal, but Katie could be done for.

Katie headed onto the roof.

The beast growled and snarled as he pulled off a piece of the wino he'd found on the roof.

He stood up and waved the human's legs like he was a conductor. He sang his own song, something classical but unrecognizable, as he tilted his head back and forth, flinging the limbs around as he directed his phantom orchestra.

"These stupid humans," he growled. "They are even weaker than I originally thought. Nothing holds them together anymore. The last time I was here they at least put up a fight, but look at this one."

He picked up the wino's head and tossed it over the edge, then chowed down on one of the legs.

"He was too drunk to move." The demon scowled as he talked to himself. "My food had incapacitated itself enough that all I had to do was walk over and eat it. Pretty stupid food."

The demon looked out over the city of San Diego, watching the heat of the sun shimmer up from the rooftops. He tossed the unfinished leg to the side and picked up an arm, figuring he might as well enjoy his food in peace. There was no other demon like him on that plane at that point, and he saw the potential the modern world offered.

A buffet lay before his eyes—not just to feed his physical appetite, but a dominion he could rule unfettered.

The people were simple, ready to do whatever it took to stay alive—that was the human way. It always had been, no matter how many centuries passed. This time, though, he would take the world for everything it was worth.

The demon stood up and wiped his mouth on the

wino's torn sleeve as if it were a napkin, then tossed it to the side with a satisfied growl. His strength was returning, and he could feel the power within him surge. He wasn't at full capacity yet, but after a few more meals he would be unstoppable.

Suddenly he sensed another more powerful demon; one above the level of his leader, even. He spun slowly and spotted the female the demon occupied. She was two buildings away, but she suddenly ran toward him at high speed. She leapt across the gap between the buildings, her eyes glaring into his.

"Oh look, home delivery!" The demon sneered.

He rubbed his massive hands together as his weight crushed the roofing material below his feet. His cold smile dripped blood as she sprinted forward, pulling one of her knives out. As he waited patiently for the girl, he heard the wailing of police sirens below him.

He growled in annoyance and moved to look over the edge of the building. As he stared at the ground, tilting his head again, a snarl left his lips.

Katie stopped in her tracks, curious as to what he was staring at. Before she could get there, though, he had leapt off the ledge.

"No," she yelled, reaching the edge just in time to see him land.

She slammed her fists on the edge, leaving broken bricks where her hands had struck. She was strong and powerful, and Pandora was giving her everything she could without taking over.

Katie looked at the buildings to find the best place to exit, but there was barely anywhere to get down without going inside and using the stairs. She didn't know what kind of backup this beast might have, and she didn't want to chance entering a building without her team.

She tapped her earpiece. "Uh, Calvin? You've got company."

"Turn here," Calvin yelled, holding onto the handle on the ceiling as the cop car squealed down an alleyway and shot back out onto the main road.

The cop backed up a bit to give them a better view of the building, and Calvin stared up at the creature on top of the building. It was a big-ass motherfucker.

"All right," Calvin began. "When I give the signal, I want you to turn on your siren for just a minute. I need to give my partner ample time to get prepared for that beast. And I... Hold on."

Calvin looked down at his phone as Korbin's came up name on the screen. He let it go to recording, since he needed to focus on not dying at that moment. Of course, because Korbin didn't play that game, he called right back.

This time Calvin picked up the phone. "I'm a little busy, boss," he said, giving them the signal to hit the siren. "We got a big one. Tracking it down, and... OH, *HOLY FUCK!*"

Calvin dropped the phone and looked up at the edge of the building, from which the beast was snarling at him with bared teeth. Calvin grabbed the phone again and put it to his ear.

"Calvin!" Korbin's irritated voice assaulted him. "What the *fuck* is going on?"

Calvin grimaced. "Boss, we got us a big-ass mother-fucker, 'kay? I need you guys to come on over and… Well, if we don't make it, it's been a good run, boss. I'll send the coordinates."

"We got 'em. Tracked 'em with your phone," Korbin replied. "Hang tight, and for fuck's sake don't die."

"Right." Calvin pressed End and looked out through the windscreen.

The demon jumped from the edge and landed in the alley the cops had used as a shortcut. When his huge legs slammed down they compacted several dumpsters, crushing them completely flat. The cement under them cracked and broke, sending small shards flying. He shook his head and took a deep breath, raising his eyebrows.

The cops were terrified. "What the fuck is that?" Stone gasped. "I don't even know who to call in."

Calvin reached out to stop Stone from grabbing the radio. "No need to call it in. We are the only ones certified to handle it. He would eat your entire squadron."

"I do not doubt you on that," Stone exclaimed, dropping his hand in his lap and staring down the alley. "What the fuck are you going to do about it?"

"Well, we have to neutralize it," Calvin told them.

Holden was incredulous. "And what the fuck does that mean?"

"I'm not really sure." Calvin shrugged. "It just seemed like the right thing to say in the moment. Ultimately we are going to have to take that motherfucker's head clean off its shoulders."

"Do you have a chainsaw?" Stone wondered.

"No," Calvin snapped. "We fight with swords."

"What are you, the Knight-fucking-brigade?" Holden asked from the back seat.

"No." Calvin sighed. "We are the Damned, and we have some pretty fucking fancy tricks up our sleeves when it comes to demons. That girl on the roof—she is a most wonderful badass. Speaking of Katie, she needs to get her ass down here."

Calvin picked up the radio and put it to his mouth.

"Hey, sweet thang," he sang. "You gonna get your ass down here, or do I have to take this motherfucker on by myself?"

"You're a big man." She giggled. "Just keep him preoccupied."

"Right," he said, dropping the radio. "'Preoccupied.' How the fuck do we keep a beast like that *preoccupied*? He could crush my body with his damn pinky. *This* is the kind of shit I was talking about. Brothers do not belong in dark alleyways beating fucking demon ass. *Fuck*."

There was nothing but silence from the cops.

Calvin turned to them with a bright smile. "So, guys, you remember how I told you that you were backup?" he asked.

They both nodded.

"Okay, so this is what that means," Calvin explained. "I'm gonna get my ass out of this car and be a mother-fucking hero. You two are going to back the hell up. You are going to back your car to the street, and not let anyone past you. Do you think that you can handle that?"

They fidgeted uncomfortably under Calvin's gaze.

"Yeah, got it," they both mumbled.

"All right," Calvin said. "Let me get out first."

Holden started to speak, then changed his mind, then spoke anyway. "Good luck," he managed thickly.

"Thank you. I'm pretty sure I'll have to make my own damn luck," Calvin retorted, throwing the door open and stepping out into the street.

Holden moved back to the front seat, pulling the passenger door closed behind him. Stone put the car in reverse and spun the tires, backing up as fast as he could. Calvin pulled out his guns and looked up at the demon, who now had his full attention on Calvin.

"All right, you goddamned bastard," Calvin said to himself. "Come get some."

9

Korbin hung up the phone and hit the emergency button to sound the red alarm. He threw off his jacket and pulled on his boots, shaking his head at the trouble the two of them constantly got themselves into.

He glanced out the office window that overlooked the pit, seeing everyone rushing down to find out what was going on. He took a deep breath and grabbed the two knives Katie gave him. He wasn't going to go out there with half a team and not prepare them.

Korbin stomped out of the office, pulling the door shut behind him, and jogged down to the pit. When he rounded the corner, he found Eric and Derek pulling on their boots. He stopped and looked at them for a minute before handing each a knife.

"Do *not* lose these," he said. "They are worth more than your fucking *lives*, boys. From what it sounded like, we are going to need all the help we can get in this battle."

Eric and Derek nodded and waited for him to walk away, high-fiving and sliding the knives into their setup as soon as Korbin's back was turned. They had watched the others fight with them, so they knew what kind of power that they held. Derek was a partner in the company, and Eric was just ready to play with the cool-as-fuck toys.

They stood there looking at each proudly, puffing out their chests with the knives on the front of their vests.

"It's about damn time!" Derek's face shone with pride. "How do I look?"

"Fucking *badass*." Eric grinned. "And me?"

"Not entirely ridiculous, like you normally do," Derek deadpanned.

"*Hell*, yeah." Eric whooped, nodding. "We gotta get new sheaths for these beauties."

"Yeah, we do." Derek smirked. "And come up with names for them."

"Mine is 'Hell-Demon Slayer.'" Eric grunted to empha-size his manliness.

"Mine is 'Theresa,'" Derek said, nodding wistfully.

Erik looked askance at him. "'*Theresa?*' Why?"

Derek had a shine in his eyes "After this waitress I met in Tulsa one time. She was a ballcrusher in *every fucking way*."

"Ohhh." Eric chuckled in understanding. "Makes perfect sense when you know the whole story."

"All right, big and ugly," Calvin said, crouching and facing the demon. "Whatcha got for me, huh? You gonna eat me too?"

"I don't like dark meat," the demon growled. "But don't worry, little black man. I'll make sure you are a real ugly stain on the cement.

"Oh, okay," he said in a high-pitched tone. "You're going for the racial slurs. Hmm. Well, let me just tell you something, Colonel-fucking-Ward—race relations are a little different from the last time you came around."

"Still black, still ignorant." The demon sneered, waving a claw toward the rooftop from which Katie watched them. "Still a slave."

"Awww, *hell* no," Calvin said, lunging for the beast and swiping his sword across his shin. "We don't have slaves anymore and Jim Crow is fucking dead, just like you are gonna be very shortly."

Calvin lunged again, this time piercing the demon's flesh with the blade. Steaming blood poured from the wound, but the beast dismissed it with a laugh. He swiped out with an arm, tossing Calvin across the alley and against a wall. Calvin groaned as he rubbed his chest.

"Damn," he whispered.

Calvin got in several more licks, but nothing like what the demon did to him.

Above them, Katie/Pandora perched on the edge, looking down at the demon below. He was huge and misshapen.

I know this demon, Pandora told her.

I thought he was your brother? Katie was confused.

Him? No, Pandora scoffed. *That's one of his cronies, the greasy little fucker.*

Katie sniffed. *He doesn't look so little to me.*

Well, I was actually talking about what he has between his legs. You know, little fucker? Pandora managed to sound both sweet and acerbic. *No?*

Katie snorted. *Tell me about him, and I don't mean his goddamned pecker.*

He is a weasel. A big one, but a rodent nonetheless, Pandora told her. *He's spent his existence chasing my brother and trying to be important, but he is nothing like him. He doesn't have the speed, power, or size my brother has.*

Well, that's fucking reassuring. Katie sighed.

My brother probably sent him here to scope things out. He's an ass. Pandora made no attempt to hide her derision. *He probably figured he could come here and play out whatever plan my brother has. He always thinks he can outsmart T'Chezz, but this guy is dumber than rocks.*

He seems to know his fair share of racist slurs, Katie snarled.

Pandora dismissed her anger. *You know how that is—he just grabbed onto whatever he thought would make him feel smart, and there is plenty of that shit in hell. Where do you think it comes from in* this *world? I mean, shit...demons have been screwing with you guys for ages. They don't really give two fucks about you, but they know if they pull you apart they can target you easier. There are all kinds of demons in your political closets.*

That doesn't really surprise me at all. Katie shook her head as she replied. *I've been saying that for years; long before I knew anything about the Damned.*

See, you knew all along! Pandora congratulated her. *We are assholes. I was in politics for a while, but it kept pissing me off how everything was for men on this planet. I went back home instead and sat on my throne with my demon child servants.*

What a lovely story about your home life, Katie gushed snarkily. *Did you have Sunday beheadings?*

Only once a month. Pandora's laughter chimed in Katie's head.

That must have been the main event, Katie snickered, watching the beast's moves. *You know, your friend down there —he isn't too bad at this, but he is mostly girth. Haven't you guys learned that agility is much better than girth, unless you are going for smashing buildings and throwing buses? The rest of the time you get screwed by the smaller, faster people.*

Pandora agreed. *I've said that for years, but my brother is pretty much composed of testosterone, so he tends to build cock diesel fuckers and then watches them die when they can't handle the weight of the suit.* Katie felt the demon's mental shrug. *But I don't give a shit. It's their funerals, coming up here and trying to take over. They seriously underestimate the humans on this planet.*

Well, don't worry about that, Katie reassured her. *That is all going to end very soon, and when it does, we need to be prepared to strike at the heart of this whole thing. I won't be bullied by some massive hunk of stinky flesh, and I won't fear for the lives of my people because those smelly monstrosities want to play puppeteer with our bodies. Fuck that!*

That's the best speech you've ever made.

I have a question for you, Katie began haltingly.

All right, Pandora replied. *Hit me with it.*

Katie winced and shook her head as Calvin took a particularly hard knock to the face. *If your dumbass brother is eventually coming for me, don't you think that we should start practicing like he is the one up here?*

I see where you are going with this, Pandora purred. *And I like every fucking bit of it.*

Katie narrowed her eyes in determination. *Then get prepared. I'm tired of this bullshit. If I need to use these powers to save my teammate and the city, Korbin will just have to deal with it.*

That's right, girl! Preach it! Pandora cheered.

There is a reason that the two of us were brought together, Katie said, stepping up on the ledge and breathing heavily. *I think it's because somebody out there knew we could kick some serious ass together.*

Amen! Pandora sang, *Ain't nobody gonna break-a my stride...*

Katie looked at the demon. *Let me ask you...what are my chances?*

I give it forty percent. Pandora sounded uncertain.

Katie pursed her lips, considering. *Ooookay, and how confident are you that I'll land where I should?*

Pandora's tone was airy. *You know I don't like to guess at those things, but think of it this way. You do it—you pull that shit off—and it will be the most epic moment. It will be one of those where if the humans win they will put it in the history books, maybe build a statue like. That kind of thing.*

Riiight. Katie let out a short chuckle. *I was more thinking a "thank you" from my teammate for saving his ass.*

That might happen too. Pandora sighed. *You humans are so boring in your aspirations.*

Because kicking ass and saving lives is so boring, Katie

retorted, pulling both her knives out and holding them to her side. *Here goes nothing.*

Katie's eye's flashed bright red and she stepped off the six-story building, falling toward the beast below.

Calvin groaned and lifted the collar of his shirt to wipe the blood from his lips. He folded it back down and looked at the front of it, which was now covered in blood. At least he had taken the jacket and tie off before he played with Demon Psycho 332, or whatever his name was.

Calvin rolled up the sleeves of his shirt. "You know, I paid like a hundred bucks for this shirt." He lifted a foot and wrinkled his nose in distaste. "Not to mention my shoes; I won't even tell you how much *they* were. Let's just say that it was Sunday church clothes kind of money on this one suit. Now you got fucking blood on it, and though my drycleaner Mrs. Wong is badass, she will frown at demon blood."

"What about *your* blood?" the demon taunted.

Calvin gritted his teeth as the demon pulled a light post out of the ground, dragging the wiring out with it. Sparks sprayed onto the ground as he tapped it in his hand like a ballplayer with his bat.

The demon turned toward Calvin, his voice oozing contempt. "I bet this will bash your puny little head in pretty well."

Calvin gave the demon a hard sneer of his own and growled, "Not that puny."

The demon hefted the pole into position over his

shoulder. "Well, you pint-sized pecker, *you* are the one bleeding, not me."

"Oh, we can change that if you would like," Calvin gibed. "I'm sure if I look hard enough I can find your demon balls to chop off and roll down the alleyway."

"It'll be hard to do that without a head," the demon countered, smashing the pole down right next to where Calvin was standing.

"You mother*fucker*!" Calvin cursed, picking himself up from the ground. "You don't like dark meat because we make you jealous."

The demon roared in anger and pulled the light post to his side again, ready to sweep the whole alleyway clear. He pulled his arm back and Calvin winced, thinking about how badly it was going to hurt.

As the demon began to swing, Katie slammed down onto the demon's shoulders. It felt to Calvin like the entire block shook from the shockwave. She landed hard and arced her arms down from behind her head, slamming her knives straight down through the demon's skull into his brain.

"Holy shit!" Calvin jumped back, shocked by what he had witnessed. "That was fucking badass."

"Thanks." Katie groaned, holding on tightly to the demon's head as he roared in pain and tromped about the alleyway.

Katie reached down and pulled her sword from her side.

"Don't be lying about on the fucking job!" she screamed into the demon's ear.

Katie used the sword to block the pole that he was still

swinging around violently. She held onto the handle of one of the knives in his head tightly and blocked several rogue advances, while the demon was screaming in pain, thrashing around, and slamming into all sorts of shit.

His head was on fire, and she had Joshua and his knives to thank for that little fact. The demon wouldn't even be halfway down by that point if it weren't for the new weapons, and she wouldn't waste the opportunity.

"*Die*, you bastard!" Katie stood back up on the beast's shoulders and pushed the knife farther into his head.

The beast groaned and bucked, not wanting to give in, not wanting to let go of the body he had found himself in on their plane of existence. The demon shifted and Katie lost her footing, slipping down his back and onto the ground.

She sheathed her sword and growled, "Fuck!"

She kept dodging the beast's maddened swipes. Calvin stood in the background, leaning against the dumpster and just watching the show.

Katie was pretty sure he was wishing for popcorn right at that moment. It probably *was* quite amusing to watch her struggle like that.

She rolled across the ground, dodging the beast's pole again, and looked up to find a path back to her knives. She ran forward and catapulted herself off the ground from the demon's arm to latch onto a handy metal pole sticking out of the wall, then turned her body, pushed off with her legs, and soared toward the demon. She grabbed her knife handles and planted her feet on his shoulders.

"Fuck you, beast," Katie growled.

No! Pandora screamed. *Don't do it!*

It was too late. Katie had twisted her knives and yanked them out of his head.

The demon's eyes began to flash, and a deep chuckle moved through his body and out of his mouth.

Katie wasn't sure what the hell was happening, but she jumped down and moved toward Calvin, looking back at the demon. He smiled one last time, and disappeared as if into thin air. Katie knitted her eyebrows together and started kicking the trash aside, looking for the demon or dust or anything that would show her where he had gone.

Pandora didn't try to hide her outrage. *Fucking hell! Great fucking job. Now he's back in hell...with my brother. This will definitely* not *be the last we fucking see of him. What the fuck! That was so damn frustrating, Katie!*

I'm sorry! Katie apologized. *I thought he would turn to dust like the others.*

You were dead wrong, Pandora grumbled, mollified.

10

"Shit." Calvin groaned as he bent over and grabbed his notebook off the ground. "My back is *killing* me. That demon kicked my fucking ass."

Katie patted him on the back, which made him flinch. "You gave him hell." She chuckled.

Everyone came in to help clean up the area, but they kept the police presence light so they'd have fewer people to try to explain everything to. The incidents were getting harder and harder to cover up, especially since the demons were now the size of the Hulk and had a nasty habit of throwing their afternoon human snacks over the sides of buildings.

"All right," Calvin announced to the assembled officers, "I need everyone to gather over here. I know a lot of you are mind-blown completely from what you saw today, and I know you have a serious desire to talk to someone about that. I get that completely, but you need to make sure the only people you talk to are the therapists specifically appointed by your police chief." He looked from face to face. "This is not a game. This can change everything, if the word gets out. Your job is to protect and serve your citizens. It is for the greater good of San Diego that this stays under the radar."

"Now," Katie added, "if you spill the beans while you are drunk at a bar or freaking out at home with the little wifey, you will have a big problem on your hands. We have the power to make sure that you don't remember a thing, and I don't mean just the event. We can wipe years of your memories. I promise you will not remember the girl you're dating, the one you just married, or the little baby you just had if you let this information slip." She softened her tone just a touch. "We are not playing here. There is a reason that the Damned don't really exist, at least not on paper. We are *enigmas*. People of the past, people who are dead to everyone who ever loved them. Our only objective is to protect *you*. We are the angels in the shadows, the ones who keep the cops safe while you officers protect everyone else."

"Think about it before you open those lips, folks," Calvin picked up the spiel. "Because we are always watching, and your faces? They are ingrained in our minds."

"I have a question." one of the officers said, raising his hand. "Can you make me forget my six-month marriage?"

Katie chuckled as she stepped forward with a butter-wouldn't-melt smile for the cocky officer.

"Yes, Officer." She made her eyes flash for a fraction of a second, just long enough to see the surprise ripple his confident expression. "It just so happens that we can."

"Okay, then," said the officer croaked, swallowing.

"I hate smartasses," Calvin grumbled.

"Calm down. They are just making light of it to deal with everything," Katie told him. "Not everyone is a super-hero like you."

"I wonder how much time we have before he comes back," Calvin said, looking up at the roof.

You have at least twenty-four hours, Pandora told them, *but after that it's up in the air. Both of you need food and rest. He won't come back the same.*

"I don't know." Katie sighed. "But I *do* know he will come back stronger than before. We should get some food and rest before that happens."

"You're right," Calvin agreed, limping toward the police car so they could get a ride to their SUV. "Come on, let's go get some donuts."

Calvin and Katie left the scene and headed to The Donut Bar, one of the best donut places in San Diego. Calvin and Katie went inside and picked out a dozen rings of sugary goodness and sat down in the corner with them and their coffee. She bit into one of the crème brûlée-stuffed donuts and felt the sugar rush into her bloodstream.

Holy hell! Pandora exclaimed. *This donut thing is fucking amazing. There is dough and sugar, and there is shit inside! How do they get it inside!*

They squirt it into the hole, Katie replied, licking the dusting of icing sugar from the tip of her finger.

Heh heh heh.

You are such a child, Katie chided. *Seriously?*

I am impressed that you caught on this time without having to be told the meaning of life," Pandora teased. "*But seriously, my life was not complete until I tried this donut. Why have you hidden this from me?*

Honestly, I don't think I have ever eaten this kind of donut, Katie confessed. *They aren't good for you, so they were off-limits for volleyball, and when I was a kid my mom didn't spend her money on things like donuts. We were too poor for shit like that. I guess because I hadn't had them often, I never thought about donuts as an adult.*

Pandora feigned a sob. *Well, we have them now, and that is all that matters.*

Okay, but we cannot eat like gluttons again. I'll get fat," Katie maintained. *"NOTHING tastes as good as skinny feels."*

Pandora didn't miss a beat. She grumbled, *Except donuts. Donuts tell skinny it can go fuck itself.*

Why do you want me to be overweight? Katie asked. *I'd move slowly. Slow people become victims. Dead people can't have demons inside them, so* you *will end up having a happy little family reunion with your brother, at least after you get out of the depths. Maybe he will bake you a fucking cake, too.*

Still might be worth another of these donuts, Pandora grumped.

Katie had to restrain herself from slapping her forehead, settling for a sigh instead. *You are hopeless, Pandora.*

"So how does it work?" Liza asked Joshua. "Do you have to say spells?"

"N-n-no," he stuttered. "All you see is the fire and the coal, right? Well, underneath this is a tunnel that moves air up and ash down. It keeps the fire burning."

"Oh," Liza remarked brightly, twirling her hair. "And then you stick the metal in *there*?"

Joshua blushed under her gaze. "Pretty much," he explained. "You have to get it to a certain temperature before you can put the metal in. Heat it up so it gets red and fiery, *then* you hit it with that hammer to shape it into what you want it to look like."

"So you don't start out with a knife like that?" Liza asked.

"No." Joshua shook his head, pulling out a fresh billet to show her. "You start with something more like this."

Liza's mouth formed a little 'o' of amazement. "Well, how do you do the small ones without burning yourself?"

Joshua had trouble meeting her eyes. "You use these long tongs," he mumbled shyly. "You grip it with these, and put it in the fire and do the same thing. When you've gotten it to the shape you want, you want to dip it into water to cool it off before the blade warps. That allows it to keep its shape. Then you move on to the other tools to get a sharp edge, and so on and so forth."

"Do you burn yourself a lot?" she wondered.

Joshua shrugged. "I did with my old forge because it was so small, but I have these big thick gloves now, so I rarely even feel the heat except on my face and my arms. We've taken a lot of precautions here to keep me safe while I'm working."

"You are the only one who can do this," Liza told him with a megawatt grin. "We wouldn't want to lose you, because then there would be no business."

"I know, right?" Joshua laughed nervously.

"Liza?" Mamacita called from the top of the stairs. "Come help me with something."

"I gotta go." She smiled and left Joshua to get on with his work.

When she reached the top of the stairs Mamacita grabbed her by the arm and led her into the office. She shut the door and looked at her angrily. Liza had no idea what she had done, but she never wanted to make Mamacita upset.

"What did I do?" she asked nervously, licking her lips.

Mamacita's expression was flat. "What were you asking Joshua?"

"I asked him how a forge worked, and how you bent the metal, and how you made the sharp part of a sword," she explained slowly.

"And that was it?"

"Yeah." She shrugged. "He explained it really well."

"Look." Mamacita leaned forward to stress her point. "I will not allow *any* of the women in our home to 'trick' Joshua into a relationship. He has a...well, an alternative personality, I will say, and he will not understand when a woman is trying to use him for something. I know you tricky bitches. You like to get yourselves into situations with men you believe will set you free. Well, Joshua is just as imprisoned as you, although he has more money in his bank account."

Liza spluttered her denial. "I don't want his money!"

Mamacita gave her a knowing smile. "Good. When you think of Joshua, I want you to think of him as *my* boy—as if he were my flesh and blood." She paused to make sure Liza was getting the message. "So if you don't want to shit my high-heels out of your ass, you'd better treat him the right way! And I don't mean giving him your sexual favors, like at the house. I mean like a real man, with feelings and a heart."

"Mamacita," Liza said, putting her hands up. "I am sure that Joshua is a fine man, and great person. He seems very sweet. But honestly, I was just interested in forging. I've always wanted to work with my hands and make things."

"Right," Mamacita said, her hands on her hips. "Well, I can give you plenty of things to work on with your hands back at the house, and then poof—magically you've made money."

"I meant something more than just turning tricks." Liza let out a heavy sigh. "Something I could really *do*, you know? Like Armani told me. He said I could do anything if I put my mind to it, and I believed him. I just have to have the right opportunity. There aren't a lot of opportunities at the house, you know? It's work most of the time, so when I am out, I try to learn new things. I didn't think of Joshua in that way at all. I just liked hearing about making different kinds of weapons. He *is* really talented."

"Hmmm." Mamacita's mouth quirked dubiously. "He is, and we are going to leave it at that. Now, if you want to help, there are floors to be swept and walls to be painted to brighten this place up a little, and then we will run and get some food. I'm sure Joshua is starting to get hungry."

Liza capitulated. "Yes, ma'am. Thank you for giving me the day off from the house and letting me work here instead. I really like it. Maybe one day I'll have a job like you, working out of an office, wearing nice clothes like your suit, and driving a car."

"I'm sure you can do it if you put your mind to it." Mamacita watched her walk away. "And someone else's, for good measure." She rolled her eyes.

Katie entered the team's San Diego house, which was situated in a smaller area outside the city proper called Imperial Beach. It was quiet there. No one asked too many questions, and they had a big place right on the water. Katie hadn't been there before, but she was more than happy to have some time in the sun and sand.

"I'm gonna go grab a shower," Calvin told her. "There are clothes—bathing suits, etc.—up in the bedrooms. Feel free to do whatever you like, but don't go far. Korbin and the team will be here soon."

"Gotcha," Katie replied, pulling up a chair. "I think I might be just fine sitting here in this chair staring out at the ocean. I'll take one later."

"It's nice, isn't it?" Calvin smiled. "I'll be back."

Katie leaned back in her chair and put her feet up on the small table in front of her. The waves washed in and out on the shore, and she watched as surfers tried to catch a wave or two. They weren't the kind of waves you saw in movies, but the surfers were having a good time. Katie couldn't help but think about how nice it would be to spend more time near the water.

Las Vegas was her home and she loved it there, but it was a desert. Even the grass had to be imported. They had created an oasis in the middle of nowhere, and sometimes it felt a bit claustrophobic.

She took in a deep breath of the salty sea air and waved at a jogger running by. There were no houses next to them, but there were plenty of people walking up and down the beach, playing games, and just enjoying the sunshine. The sun was so warm that Katie closed her eyes. Before she knew it, she woke to the sound of Korbin barking orders at everyone else. She smiled and stretched her arms, looking into the house at the team set up.

"Hey there, sleepy head." Korbin chuckled. "Come on in and get some food, and we can talk."

"Sounds good to me." She smiled, getting up out of her chair and heading inside to help.

They had picked up a stack of pizzas and a couple of six-packs of soda on the way over, figuring no one would feel like cooking at that point. Everyone grabbed their food and headed to the porch while Korbin, Calvin, Damian, and Katie sat at the table inside. Korbin wanted to know what the hell had happened.

Pandora bitched that there were no Chicken McNuggets.

"He came out of nowhere," Calvin began in a low voice. "Someone brought that demon into this world, left it there with food, and walked out the door. Honestly, if it hadn't been for Katie I'd probably be dead. He was almost too much for one person to handle, then here comes fucking *Katie* from the goddamn *sky*. She landed on the thing and jammed both her knives into its skull."

Korbin looked to her for confirmation. "You flew from the sky?"

Katie chuckled and raised an eyebrow. "I wouldn't say I *flew*."

"Yeah, she jumped from the adjacent building," Calvin revealed. "It was badass."

"It wasn't *that* badass," Katie protested when Korbin raised his eyebrows at her. "I had gone to the roof after the demon, but when he jumped off the building I headed inside and took the stairs down aways first. When it was clear and I was good to go I jumped, and I got lucky where I landed. I mean, you didn't think I jumped from six floors up, right?"

Korbin laughed. "No, that would be nuts."

Everyone laughed, but Katie could tell that Korbin wasn't buying her story. She shrugged and took a big bite of her pizza.

She'd done what she had to do.

11

"Wakey wakey," Damian sang, sitting on the edge of Katie's bed.

"Huh?" she mumbled, then groaned and peeled an eye open to glare at him. "But it's so early."

"Early bird catches the demons." Damian's tone was serious. "Come on, I'm taking you out."

"Okay, just give me a minute," she bitched, rolling out of the bed.

"I'll be in the living room waiting for you." Damian smiled as he left the room.

That priest fucking needs to learn about personal space, Pandora drawled.

That is rich, coming from you, Katie snarked.

Katie grabbed some clothes from the closet and pulled them on hurriedly, then she headed out to the living room to meet up with Damian. He smiled and handed her a travel mug of coffee, and the two went out and jumped in one of the SUVs.

She sat quietly in the passenger seat watching the ocean waves from the window as they drove along. Damian headed away from the marina and back into the city. They pulled into the parking area of a large old church constructed of beautiful blocks of hand-carved stone. It was simple, but related so much by its age and the way that it had been preserved. He smiled and nodded as he climbed out of the car and led her inside. There was no service going on, it was just quiet. Serene like the chapel at the base in Las Vegas, only much bigger.

Katie smiled and looked around, stopping to study the intricate carvings fixed into the archways throughout the church. There were cherubs, demons, crosses, and doves in every corner of the place.

Sunlight pouring through the stained glass in the windows cascaded over the interior, washing a shifting rainbow of colors over the entire church. It was quiet there, but not awkwardly quiet—just a comfortable peace inside.

Pandora broke the spell. *Comfortable peace unless you are an altar boy.* She snickered. *I bet those doves mean something different to you when you are one of those kids. Everyone wants to give demons such a bad name, but they can't even control their own churches. I swear, humans are hypocrites of the worst kind.*

They can be, Katie agreed softly, *but humans can be beautiful creatures of light and love as well, and way more often. I haven't seen that side of any of your kind yet.*

Probably because we are dark souls. Pandora sniffed. *Light hurts my eyes.*

You mean my *eyes.* Katie laughed.

Wait, do you smell that? Pandora interrupted. *It's weed!*

Somebody is up in this church; rolling a blunt. Maybe we should move to California, if weed is part of the religious ceremonies. Hell, I'd go to church for that.

You would be hissing in the corner, Katie teased. *Can you imagine us going to church every day?*

NO! It would be miserable, but with weed...well, it could be way more interesting, Pandora insisted. *We could count our Hail Marys on cheese balls instead of on rosaries.*

Katie snickered and walked to the front of the church, where Damian was sitting. He was quiet and seemed contemplative, just staring at the candles and the brightly-colored shadows. Katie sat down next to him and let out a deep breath.

"My first experience with the church was something like this. Just sitting alone in a quiet church, reflecting," he told her. "I loved it. It was beautiful."

"That's nice." Katie smiled. "I used to go to church with my grandma, but it never really caught on for me."

"Everyone has their own spiritual journey, whether through a deity, the universe, or time spent in introspection," he said. "It's the conviction that matters in the end, or at least, that's what I think."

Katie wasn't so sure. "I hope you're right."

Damian gave her a sympathetic half-smile. "So, you want to talk about that fight yesterday? Seeing as we are in the sanctity of the church and all."

She peered at him but his eyes didn't waver, nor did the all-knowing-smile on his face. She raised her hands in the air. "You got me," she confessed. "I did jump from the top of the building. I mean, I was concerned for Calvin, and didn't realize just how high I was. Thankfully the demon was squishy."

Damian narrowed his eyes, but said nothing. He could tell she wasn't ready to tell the whole truth, and that was okay. It was up to her when she decided she was ready.

When they left, Katie noticed a marijuana store close to the church.

I don't think the smoke you smelled earlier was in the church, Katie told Pandora, glancing at the storefront.

Damn it! Pandora sighed. *Dreams...crushed.*

"You want to get some breakfast?" Damian offered as he climbed into the truck.

"Sure," Katie agreed. "Wherever you want to go."

Damian grinned. "I know just the place."

Come on, please let it be fucking donuts, Pandora begged. *Please, please, please, I'll be a good girl.*

I don't think it works the same way when you *pray.* Katie smirked.

It would if you weren't such a bitch, Pandora growled.

Damian took Katie—and Pandora—to a diner along the boulevard in Coronado, which was on their way back to Imperial Beach. The place was cute, like a real old-time diner, only it was crazy busy.

They waited nearly an hour to get a table, but Damian assured her that there weren't any other places for her to get food that they could get in and out of. It wasn't like Las Vegas. So, they stayed, and in the end Katie was glad they had.

They just had a normal conversation while eating eggs, bacon, and toast and watching the tourists come in and out, talking about the next steps when they got back to Las

Vegas. It almost felt like they were on vacation, and it would have been the first vacation Katie had ever been on.

Pandora was happy with the breakfast once Katie started eating it, so she kept quiet and let them have a decent conversation. Katie needed it, especially with everything going on.

As they were driving back from breakfast, Katie spied an occult shop on the righthand side of the street. It wasn't bright or touristy, so she could tell that it was for serious followers and researchers. She felt weird asking the priest to stop, but there were things she needed to find out about.

"Hey, is there any way you could drop me off here?" Katie asked. "There was a shop back there that I would really love to check out."

"Sure," Damian said. "You want me to come?"

"No, it's okay," she told the priest as he pulled over. "I'll just call an Uber when I am done."

Concern crossed Damian's features. "You're sure?"

She gave him a warm smile. "I'm sure. Thanks for breakfast, and confession."

"No problem," he replied. "I'll see you back at the house later today."

"I'll be there," Katie told him, shutting the SUV's door.

"Katie," Damian called before she left, doing something in his lap. "Here. You need the address for the house."

"*Duh!*" she exclaimed, shaking her head and reaching through the window to take the slip of paper he'd hastily scribbled the address on. "Thank you. I'd be wandering around for the next week trying to find the house."

As he rolled up the window she stepped onto the curb and waited there for a moment, smiling and waving as he drove away. Once he was out of sight, she pulled down her sunglasses and walked quickly across the street and up to the shop's door.

Once inside, she removed her glasses so she could check out the layout. The space was cramped, overfull, and *very* dark. They had low lighting, with candles lit all over the room. The girl behind the counter smiled as she walked in. She was pretty, with long black hair, very short bangs, bright red lipstick, and a nose piercing. Katie pulled her bag around in front of her and wandered through the shop, taking everything in.

In one back corner was a rare book section with a comfortable chair and some bottled water. She pulled down a couple of books, and sat there reading about different things having to do with the occult.

In essence, the books described the occult as knowledge of the hidden, knowledge of the immeasurable, and knowledge of the paranormal. However, the farther she read, the more she began to understand that there were both light and dark in the occult.

Her heart fell as she realized that her life was completely submerged in the dark side of things.

You have to understand that humans have done terrible things through the ages, Pandora told her. *People of the occult, demons, spirits—we are harshly judged by humans, but you are the reason that we can't openly practice, why we can't coexist. Hell, you are even the reason the planet is so fucked up and the climate is spinning out of control. Sometimes it is hard to really pinpoint who's worse in this scenario.*

Are you done doing PR for your side?

Pandora sniffed. *Only telling the truth.*

Totally objective truth, too.

See? Pandora's voice brightened. *You get it!*

I get that you are a totally biased source, like most of our news channels today. Katie told her. She noticed a noise, and turned to see someone stepping around the corner.

"Are you finding everything okay?" the girl from the front asked.

"I am, thank you," Katie assured her, then stood up to call her back. "Actually, I have a question."

"Sure." The shop girl smiled. "My name is Alice, and I own the store."

"Oh, nice." Katie returned Alice's smile and held out a hand. "I'm Katie, nice to meet you. I was wondering if there was any way that I could get any copies of old grimoires or history books?" She indicated the selection of books she'd been flicking through.

"I am looking for anything real or even *sort* of real—I have a very good nose for sniffing out good versus garbage. I just want to get enough information to fully understand some of the things in my life that have to do with the occult and some practices."

Alice nodded and smiled. "Sure. Do you live here?"

"I mostly live in Las Vegas, but I come here for business," Katie replied.

"That's not a problem. I can always mail them to you," Alice assured her. "Why don't you write your number down for me?" She fished a notepad and pen out of her pocket and passed them to Katie. "I'll do some research and call you with what I find."

"That sounds fantastic." Katie smiled. "Thank you so much. And I love your store. It's really well laid out. I could sit here all day."

Alice nodded. "That was the point of it. I wanted anyone and everyone to feel comfortable coming into my store and staying a while."

"Well, I think you accomplished that."

She ordered herself an Uber, then bought a couple of small things from the store to support the girl's business while she waited for pickup. Her mind turned over everything that she had read, and when her Uber got there she didn't even think about who was driving the thing.

She gave the driver her address and sat back, thinking about all the things she had learned that day.

That was a good day, she told Pandora. *I got a lot of questions answered.*

Pandora had other considerations. *I think you should stop thinking about books and look at the* man *driving you the hell around today in your Uber. He is so fucking hot. Like "do him right here in this car" hot.*

Katie looked at the driver for a moment and had to hold back a laugh.

What? Pandora snickered. *You* can *see him, right? Or has all that reading affected your eyesight?*

Katie giggled, drawing an odd look from the driver. *I don't think he would be interested in either of us if the gay pride flags all over the front of his car are anything to go by.*

Wait...what? Nooooooooooooo! Pandora's excitement melted. *This is total bullshit!*

Katie laughed, inwardly this time. *I don't think he would feel that way.*

No! Pandora's indignant reply rang out in Katie's head. *He's too hot to not be mine! Fuck this, I can be a guy! No, really! I can buy a strap-on, and he won't even notice the difference.*

I'm pretty sure he would, Katie told her.

Katie listened to Pandora concoct ways to make the driver straight again all the way back to the house. The demon was relentless; she obviously did not understand what it meant to be gay. She could not successfully pose as a man.

Seriously, I could get that boy's head back on straight, at least for a night....or ten, she finally declared.

Katie was so mortified about the whole thing that even though the driver couldn't hear it, she tipped him double the fare, unable to meet his eyes. Pandora carried on listing the things she'd like to do to the Uber driver.

Sometimes life with a demon inside was enough to test the patience of a saint.

And if not a saint, well, then certainly Katie.

12

The next day was back to business for everyone. Katie had to admit it was hard to think about working when you were in a place like San Diego, California.

It was freaking beautiful every day, the weather was amazing, and everyone had fallen in love with Katy's Coffee, the intimate coffee shop they'd discovered on Imperial Beach. The owner was usually to be found serving everyone from behind the counter, and there was constantly sand on the floor from the beach behind them, which added to the relaxed vibe of the establishment.

But all good things come to end, and that ending started over morning coffee with Korbin, Calvin, Damian, and herself.

Korbin hadn't been at the event and hadn't seen the demon, so he didn't know what to do with the teams—which made him grouchy.

They were trying to decide if everyone should stay in

San Diego or if he should split them up. Katie was glad Korbin was too preoccupied to notice that her mind was lost in so many other things.

Damian had noticed Korbin's mood too, and he was pushing to have the team stay.

Calvin played Devil's advocate. "I don't know," he said, considering. "I mean, we can't get that lucky *twice* with a demon like that, so it would be good to have the team here in case he comes back with a vengeance. But at the same time, the likelihood of it happening again is pretty slim. You guys have a lot to get done, and other areas to protect out there."

I just want to point out that the demon you fought was just three levels below one of the Seventy-Two, Pandora cut in. *He was extremely powerful, and that doesn't even count the fact that there are three levels above his.*

"Right," Katie said, ignoring Pandora for the moment. "But we won't be here that much longer, right?"

"Enough time to get some intel on what is going on," Korbin prompted. "Enough time to make things work and make sure it is safe out here for the people."

"Okay," Katie said, sitting back in her chair.

"I just don't know if I feel comfortable leaving the two of them to fend for themselves if this beast or another one comes back," Damian said.

I'll tell you this much, Katie, Pandora chimed in. *If you are not going to divulge what I can do and how we work together, you better have at least two more as backup. You can't keep jumping off five- or six-story buildings and expect it to go unnoticed. The priest already knows you are full of shit, Derek has seen your badassery, Korbin suspects, and Calvin...* She snorted. *Well, Calvin is oblivious. He probably wouldn't notice if you sprouted batwings and horns.*

Pandora's voice became serious. *But Katie, you are flirting with the truth here and if you aren't ready to face the repercussions for coming out with that truth then I suggest that you start covering your ass better.*

Look, Katie hissed at Pandora. *I know you think you're helping here—I get it. But what you are suggesting is impossible! I can't just request that two more people out of a seven-man total team stay here and not tell them why I need them. In order to keep our secret, we will have to take some risks. We will have to face some of these demons on our own, and hope for the best.* She sighed mentally. *I want to be back in Las Vegas just for the safety in numbers, but we can't go back until we find out where this demon came from, and who summoned him and why. The only question is whether the rest of the team will be there next time I jump from a six-story building and receive nothing, not even a scratch.*

All right, fine, Pandora huffed. *But next time* don't take the knives out of his fucking head! *With the knives in there he can't leave this dimension, nor can he even start to try to think straight. Seriously, what the fuck possessed you to pull your knives back out?*

"*He was going crazy,*" Katie retorted in her own defense. *He was going nuts, and I was just trying to make him go away like I had done with every other demon. I did not know that he wouldn't turn to dust. I didn't know he would just return to Hell, either. It would have been nice if you had told me in the first damn place.*"

Pandora's silence spoke volumes.

That's what I thought, Katie snarked, refocusing on the conversation at the table.

Korbin was waving a hand in front of her face. "Earth to Katie!"

She smiled apologetically. "Sorry, Korbin. Train of thought ran away with me still on it. What were you saying?"

Korbin gave her a disapproving shake of his head. "I was asking where you think this demon came from."

"I think it was someone here," Katie speculated. "Someone who has knowledge of the area and the kind of demon they were summoning." She took a sip of her tea and made a face at the tepid brew. "They purposely trapped the demon in that circle with a fuse, which gave them five or ten minutes to load up and get the hell out of there. They knew they didn't want to be anywhere *near* that demon when he got out, therefore they knew how dangerous he was."

Korbin considered her theory and nodded. "So, it's an inside man, and an inside job," he repeated. "Right, so in order to even start to understand what was going on, we need to figure out who this inside guy is and then go from there. It sounds like detective work." He grimaced at the thought. "Okay, here's what we're going to do: Calvin and Katie are going to stay and meet up with the reporter, and everyone else will come back to Vegas for now." He held up a hand before Calvin could argue. "We have a jet, Calvin. It's a short flight, and we can get back here fast if we need to. I think that you guys are going to be fine as far as demons are concerned. You just need to get to that reporter before someone else does. Every minute you're not there protecting her could be her last."

Katie blanched at the thought.

Korbin gave her a stoic nod. "Remember, you have to keep her safe. If that means bringing her back to the beach house, do it. This isn't like the base with all our secret stuff. It's just a safehouse that we can protect."

"Yes, sir," Katie said.

"One last thing, Katie. Keep your feet on the ground from now on." He chuckled. "No more launching yourself from the top of six-story buildings, and that's an order." He turned his attention to Calvin. "And *you*. The next time I call, you'd better answer the first time around."

Calvin snapped a salute. "Yes, sir!" He grinned. "I'll put Groth the megademon on the line with you next time, sir. Maybe you guys can chat about cooking and swap some recipes."

"Smart ass." Korbin scowled and stood up. "All right, Damian, let's get the team ready and packed up. We need to get back to Vegas and continue training."

Katie remained at the table with Calvin, her mouth firmly shut. The rest of the team was bummed to leave, but they dragged themselves into the house to get ready. Katie just wanted to get the whole thing over with, in and out.

She stood up and went out on the porch to watch the ocean until it was time. There would be no reporter-flavored takeout for the demons today—not on *her* watch.

Calvin sat at the table for a while after the team left,

allowing the stress of the last two days to evaporate with the foam on his coffee.

He tried to wrap his mind around what they were about to do.

They hadn't had a chance to develop the non-martial skills they would need for this assignment. Usually being a Damned meant fighting demons, and that was about it. For the first time since he had been there, they had to do some investigative work. He wasn't sure if that was a good thing, or if they should be worried that it signified things were getting worse out there.

Katie went back inside after the last of the staff vehicles left in a puff of exhaust fumes. She found Calvin at the table and joined him. They sat there in silence for several minutes, thinking about the task at hand.

Finally Katie turned to Calvin. "OK, we have the reporter's schedule, thanks to your research. So how are we going to do this?" she asked. "I'm not going in without a plan. That's the perfect way to get us all killed."

"No, I have a play," Calvin assured her. "It's something I used to do before I joined Korbin's Killers."

Katie felt the corner of her mouth rise of its own free will. "Lay it on me."

Calvin grinned. "It's like this. We are going to find Charlotte first; find out what she is doing, where she is working. When we have her location, we'll send her a text to let her know we will be calling in three minutes. We will tell her that when we call she must step outside for privacy. She will do that, and we will grab her. *We* control the situation, *she* will be safe, and then we go get donuts somewhere without worrying that we are being followed or set up."

Katie slapped the table. "That plan is perfect." She laughed. "You are a *genius*!"

Pandora was in agreement for once. *Uh, yes, because of donuts. I promise that I will be on my best behavior—as long as you promise to eat another of those cream things.*

You'd better be. Katie chuckled.

"It *will* be perfect, if she isn't familiar with the scheme," Calvin commented. "I'm thinking that because she knows us, she will be okay with what we propose. I don't think she'll question it, basically."

"Right," Katie agreed. "Well, let's get rock-n-rollin'."

Katie and Calvin went to their rooms and got dressed for their day. They first went to where Charlotte lived, but she wasn't there so they talked to a couple of people who seemed to know what she did on a regular basis.

She was a reporter for the crazy side, yet she didn't change up her schedule. Katie figured she would have a talk with her later about safety, but for their purposes it worked out. They wouldn't have to chase her all over creation.

Charlotte looked down at her laptop and sighed. Another shitty article, another shitty week, and no break in any of the real cases. She had just gotten back from following the teams around on the East Coast, and figured a little time back in San Diego was best for her right now.

Still, she was getting really tired of dealing with stupid-ass people who saw Jesus in the water spot on their ceiling. At least she was working from Starbucks today. The coffee wasn't good, but it was strong and plentiful.

She pressed Enter, which sent her latest fluff piece to the editor. Just as she picked up her coffee, her phone buzzed. It was a text message from a number she didn't recognize.

Charlotte. It's Calvin from the Las Vegas team. I'm in the area and you've been asking for an interview, so here I am. I am going to call you in one minute. I need you to take your things and go outside to accept the call. It will keep us both safe.

She pulled her brows together and shook her head, dismissing the gut feeling she had. She was really surprised to be getting a call from one of the Damned. They never talked to anyone, and she had been trying unsuccessfully to sit down with them for a long-assed while now.

Something felt off about the whole thing, but at the same time she couldn't let her suspicious nature get in the way of an interview with one of *them*. She grabbed her stuff, shoved it in her bag, and headed out of the coffee shop. She walked away from the store and in front of the alley way. The phone rang, and she hit Answer.

"Hello?"

A deep, calm voice spoke. "Charlotte, this is Calvin. Don't be scared."

She stiffened. "What?"

It was too late.

A hand cupped her mouth and her assailant pulled her into the alley, where she was thrust into an SUV. The man in the driver's seat, who she assumed was Calvin, looked back and nodded as they took off.

Charlotte sat up straight in the seat and looked at the woman who had taken her, and at Calvin. She flushed with simultaneous fear and anger.

"Who *are* you, and what are you doing with me?" she snapped, glaring at the woman.

The woman held out a hand. "I'm Katie. Look, I'm sorry we had to do it that way, Charlotte. We know who you are, and what you are trying to do. We need to talk, but we need to do it on our terms. You are in danger. It wouldn't be the first time someone from your profession dug too deeply into a story and found themselves standing in their own grave. We know you have been looking into us for a long time—and we don't blame you for that—but we hide information to protect you from harm."

"I wasn't going to call for help, or whatever," Charlotte snapped.

Katie raised an eyebrow at her.

"Okay, fine, that was *exactly* what I would have tried to do," she admitted. "But do you blame me? You dragged me into an alley, threw me into a blacked-out SUV, and took off for God-knows-where. Where *are* we going, by the way?"

Katie narrowed her eyes at the reporter and dropped her voice. "Somewhere dastardly. Scary. *Evil*, even."

Charlotte's eyes widened, but she managed to squeak, "Where?"

Katie lifted a single eyebrow. "We're going…to get some donuts."

"Oh!" Charlotte tittered in relief. "Okay, I get it. You wanted to make sure you were safe, I was safe, and that I couldn't screw you over."

"Yep," Katie said.

Charlotte took a closer look at Katie. "Hey, aren't you the girl who was rescued from the parking garage incident back in Las Vegas?"

"In the flesh," Katie replied, raising her chin toward the reporter.

"Well, you look better in person," she told her. "*Way* more badass."

Katie snickered, shaking her head. She supposed that maybe she *had* become a bit of a badass. It was out of necessity, though, and she still felt bad for kidnapping this girl, even if she was trying to spill the beans on their clandestine organization.

"Do you like donuts?" Katie asked.

"Umm, who *doesn't* like donuts?" Charlotte countered.

I like this girl already, Pandora purred. *Maybe I should switch bodies.*

Okay, but she will write an expose on your life, Katie warned her. *You will forever be the reporter's demon, recounting stories for the next piece she needs to write. Each story will get you a donut.*

Oh, hell *no,* Pandora spat. *Let's just stick with donuts and demon killings.*

Good choice. Katie laughed. *Good choice.*

13

Korbin sat at his desk, rubbing his chin as he tried to figure out what was going on.

Things had changed, and it wasn't for the better. What had happened with Katie and Calvin in San Diego was alarming, to say the least.

The demons they had been facing to that point had all been controllable from inside a human. They couldn't survive outside. This demon, though, didn't need a human body for anything other than food, and from what it sounded like, the demon grew stronger with every human it swallowed. This was not something he could keep to himself, and it was obvious that things were getting darker by the second.

When Korbin had gotten back from San Diego, he had scheduled a conference call with the heads of the other teams on his side of the states: Brian Hudson, William Hunt, and Amy Brown.

He knew they would all make themselves available,

since he rarely called emergency meetings. In fact, he was usually the guy who trudged in at the last second to those types of meetings. He looked at the clock and called into the meeting service, entering the chat room and putting the phone on speaker.

"Hello?" Korbin asked.

"Yes, Korbin," Amy answered. "We are all here. What is going on?"

"I'm sure that by now you guys have heard there was an incursion of sorts in San Diego," he began.

"We heard something about it," William replied. "Sounded like the demon gave your team a run for its money."

"He did," Korbin agreed. "But that isn't really the concern."

"Then what is?" Amy asked.

"The demon came over without a host body," Korbin told them.

"*What?*" Brian exclaimed. "The demon was in the flesh, just walking around San Diego?"

"Yeah," Korbin replied. "though I would have to say it was more like he was roof dwelling and chewing on corpses."

Amy gasped. "Jesus! This is not good; not good at all. What did you do?"

"Well, my team was able to get their blades into his skull, though one of them almost died doing it," Korbin replied. "But we learned that if demons at this level are fatally wounded, they go back to hell. They just disappear from our realm."

"Great," Brian grumbled. "So you only had two of your

team members on this thing?"

"Katie and Calvin were out there doing some research for me," Korbin explained. "They just happened to be around when the SD police called."

"The police?" William queried. "How did they know about us?"

"The higher-ups have given permission for us to work with the local departments," Korbin relayed. "Go to the chiefs of police and bring them in on our plans. It provides more back up; more cover, basically, for the fights."

"So you had this help on the scene there?" Amy asked.

"Yeah, pretty much the whole force was there, and while they don't seem to be too good at keeping the secret among themselves, they had no issues with not telling anyone outside the force," Korbin replied. "Of course, the thing seems so fantastical to people who aren't us that they probably are afraid of looking like nutbags."

"Shit, I feel like a nutbag most days just thinking about the truth." Brian chuckled. "As far as the cops, I just don't know. I feel like they would be a liability, not only for the teams remaining hidden, but keeping the team in play focused on getting the job done, rather than saving the cops from whatever situation they are in."

"I tend to agree," Amy remarked. "I mean, the government as a whole has been a pain in the ass to involve in anything. Everyone in there has a serious complex and they're constantly measuring dicks, when all they really do is push paper and bandage paper cuts."

"I don't know if that's fair." Korbin chuckled. "A lot of good ex-agents end up here as Damned."

"That is my point exactly," Amy told him.

"All right, I hear you," Korbin replied. "But with this new enemy on our hands and no real idea of just how many will be showing up next, I think it's important for us to surround ourselves with as many people as possible, Damned or not."

"Maybe you're right." Amy sighed. "Not happy about it, but needs must and all that."

"I personally don't have a problem with getting the Feds involved," William responded. "Just more eyes on the prize."

"Exactly," Korbin agreed. "The more people who have our backs in this situation, the better. I am dead serious about this. This is not your run-of-the-mill demon. From what I've been told, the one Calvin and Katie faced was just three levels below one of the Seventy-Two."

"Well, fuck," Amy spat. "I'm going to contact the government groups out here, and invest in more weapons while I'm at it. We will make sure to be stacked before we even think of leaving the base on a call."

"I'll do the same thing." Brian sighed.

"If you think it's the way we should go, then so will I," William replied.

"Good," Korbin said. "We need to keep our heads on straight, and be overly watchful."

With his call over, Korbin sat in his office watching the others training below. As the head of the team he wasn't just responsible for protecting the team from demons, but from the scrutiny of the outside world as well.

As soon as the government was told, he might have different entities knocking down their doors and demanding inspections, walk-throughs, and a better understanding of what was happening.

This was not a good thing. The members of his team had already given up so much. They'd had their lives ripped apart, and the last thing they needed was some politician breathing down their necks.

To top it all off, they had their business to worry about. The creation of a tool, a weapon, has infinite possibilities. In the wrong hands, this kind of weapon could be used to cause an incredible amount of pain for those it was not intended for.

Korbin did not want this technological—and perhaps mystical—advance to fall into the hands of politicians.

He wiped his face and got up from his chair, secured his knives, and headed for the building next door.

He stared through the open iron gates at the grounds. There had to be something he could do to hide the facility; make it look unassuming and unused.

He knew that he had to keep the government away, or their secret weapons wouldn't be so secret.

Or theirs.

He stared at the massive brick building and filed through ideas, each seeming more ridiculous than the one before. How in the world was he supposed to hide a huge building right next to his own?

He was starting to think that installing the company right there on the base had been a terrible idea. He had just wanted to keep it close, though, and had not seen the invasion of demons in the flesh becoming an issue, at least not that quickly.

As he took a step forward, he dragged the toe of his boot through the gravel. When he looked up, he stopped to watch a very attractive businesswoman go into the building. Her clothes were perfectly pressed and her hair was tied back neatly, and though she was too far away to make out the face, she seemed pretty damned professional.

Seeing her was a surprise, but he figured since she was carrying several boxes that had been left on the doorstep and had walked straight in, Katie or Derek had hired her to work there.

Korbin took a step forward, intending to go find out who she was, but as he started forward his phone buzzed in his pocket.

He pulled it out, seeing a reminder on his calendar for another conference call, this time with the higher-ups. He sighed, shoved his phone back in his pocket, and shrugged.

He had too much going on to be chasing a sexy pair of legs anyway.

"So tell us, what exactly have you figured out?" Katie asked, looking down with embarrassment at the sheer number of donuts on her plate.

Don't be embarrassed, sweet cheeks. This is what we live for, Pandora said.

"Well, it's both simple and complicated at the same time," Charlotte began. "On the one hand I have uncovered some seriously hidden stuff, but on the other hand, I can't seem to get close enough to them to solidify the evidence."

"You mean with photos and statements?" Calvin asked.

"Right," Charlotte confirmed.

"And by the way, this is all off the record," Calvin replied. "So you can take your finger off that recorder in your pocket."

Charlotte sighed and sheepishly pulled a voice recorder from the pocket of her sweatshirt. She clicked it off and slid it across the table with an annoyed smile on her face.

Calvin smirked and glanced at Katie, who was staring down at her donuts with lust. Calvin elbowed her and frowned. Katie sighed and looked at Charlotte.

"So tell me," Katie asked, "what makes you so sure then that these 'teams' exist."

"I've seen it with my own eyes," she said, opening her notebook. "I've written down accounts of everything, but unfortunately, without a corroborating witness and photos none of that really matters."

Katie looked at her notebook, the same kind you bought as a kid to write in during English. There were notes, sketches, and quotes scribbled on every page. There was a crease down the middle of the pages, and the notebook itself looked as if it had been folded in half and shoved into her back pocket more than once.

"All right." Calvin smiled. "Tell us what you know...or think you know."

"Okay, so I have five teams nailed down," she related. "Korbin, Amy, William, Brian, and one team only known for their insignia, which is a skull with red eyes."

Calvin tipped his head, knowing that the last on the list

was completely false. There might have been some vigilante group out there with that insignia, but they had no connection to the Killers.

He didn't want to give anything away, though, so he didn't correct her. He hoped she'd go after that one, which would lead her far from the others and also out of danger.

"What makes you so obsessed with this?" Katie asked.

"Besides the fact that the Earth is being overrun by flesh-eating demons?" Charlotte whispered, looking around. "My aunt...she made me curious."

"What does your aunt have to do with this?" Calvin asked.

"She just disappeared, and when I looked into it, it was like she had just dropped off the face of the planet," Charlotte said. "There was no body, no nothing—just a government filing that she had been killed in an accident. It didn't make any sense, and when I tried to talk to the police about it they gave all kinds of excuses but *no* real answers."

"I'm sorry about your aunt." Calvin took a bite of his donut. "But there are any number of reasons she could be missing." He waved his donut around in a circle. "Magical demon-slaying teams being at the very bottom of the list. Maybe she *did* die, and maybe it really was just an accident. We humans have a tendency to want to know why, but sometimes there just isn't an answer."

"I get that," Charlotte agreed. "But there was no body, no answers, and no investigation—just a letter from the government."

Katie started to wonder if it had been the same with her. Had her mother just one day gotten a letter from the government declaring her dead? She pondered what effect that had had on her mom. She started to understand why Charlotte would try to hunt her aunt down.

"What was her name?" Katie asked.

"My aunt?" Charlotte replied.

Katie politely didn't ask if her hearing was faulty. "Yes. What was her name, and what did she do for a living?"

"Her name was Chloe Perry," Charlotte replied. "She was an interior designer here in San Diego, and she had a very good business. No kids and no husband, but she was one of the happiest people I had ever known. The government report said she had been in an accident on the other side of town, like a mugging, but she would have had no reason to be over there and there were no pictures taken of the event or the body. We were provided a bag of ashes and a check, that was it."

"All right, here is the deal." Calvin leaned over the table, then pulled back and made a face, wiping donut sugar off the table before laying a napkin on it so he could lean forward once more. "Charlotte, we need your help and your superb research abilities. In return for helping us— and not disclosing anything—I will personally try to find out if Chloe Perry is still alive. I have contacts who can help. We will need you to look into some things for us, and in return we will work to keep you safe."

"Well," Charlotte looked at them suspiciously, "all right, but only if you really try to find out about my aunt."

"You have my word." Calvin reached over to shake Charlotte's hand.

Before they left the donut shop Katie packed hers to go, knowing Pandora would kill her if she didn't. They rode back to that same Starbucks quietly, everyone's minds going in different directions. Calvin pulled up in the same alley and nodded at Charlotte as she climbed out of the vehicle. She clutched her things, and looked the worse for wear. When she was out of earshot, Katie turned to Calvin with anger in her eyes.

"I know that we are *supposed* to achieve this directive no matter what." Katie pointed to where Charlotte had just disappeared. "But I think it's despicable to play with some- one's emotions over a loved one who has obviously either disappeared for a reason or really did die in some tragic accident. I really thought more of you than that, Calvin, especially since this is a promise you know you might not be able to keep."

"No," he said, shaking his head. "This is one promise that I actually *can* keep."

"How?" Katie asked.

"Because Chloe Perry is the team second on Hudson's Hitmen in the upper Northwest," Calvin said. "They stand by and wait for orders—they're back-up—but they are taken care of like we are, with bases and training. They are kind of a last resort, a final blow to the demons if we need it. She's right there in front of Charlotte's nose."

Katie took that in, then dropped her eyes. "I'm sorry," she got out, and Calvin waved a hand in her direction. "No, I was a bitch. I should have known better."

Calvin nodded and told her, "Next time *you* pay for the donuts."

Sitting on a bench at a park overlooking the water would normally be a serene event. Something that would calm and relax you, let you feel the ocean breeze and hear the squawking of the seagulls and the crashing of the waves. Make you feel the presence of the Earth around you.

For Katie though, it was a time to shove donuts into her mouth while hoping Pandora would maintain radio silence.

At least for one more damned moment.

Instead, the demon in her mind moaned as she worked her way through the pastries. Calvin looked at her and lifted an eyebrow.

"What?" she said through a full mouth, spewing crumbs. "I'm hungry, and my demon is a glutton."

"It's so crazy to me that you guys share pretty much everything." He smiled. "It's like you have a partner inside."

"I wouldn't call her a partner so much as a hostage-taker." Katie covered her stomach with a hand and groaned. "But it could be worse. At least she gives me some badass power behind my kicks—though I haven't revealed that to Korbin yet. I don't know how he would feel about it."

"Change is hard," Calvin ruminated, looking at the ocean. "But with the current situation, this evolution of your relationship may be what is needed to take these beasts down."

"Not all of them will be on board with that idea, I'm sure," Katie said.

"I suppose not." Calvin sighed. "My demon... He's a Nickar, though I don't know how he found himself so far from the water. Maybe that is why I love San Diego so much more now."

"What's a Nickar?" Katie asked.

"A sea demon. They are water demons, best known for drownings, capsized boats, etc.," he answered. "He is like a Level Four or something, but just sits quietly most of the time. He does keep me thirsty."

"I see." Katie smiled.

"Do you think..." Calvin began, turning toward her and pausing. "Do you think your demon could persuade him to give me some support? I know that's an unusual request, but I thought maybe it was worth a try. That last demon would have killed me, no doubt."

What do you say? Katie asked Pandora.

How very demon-like of you to ask the other side to help defeat themselves, Pandora grumbled. *He* does *realize that as demons we use pain and torture while you meatsacks use friendship, soap operas, and donuts?*

We do what we can. Katie laughed. *What do you say?*

I might be able to, she snapped. *But you are going to have to negotiate with me.*

Katie sighed. *I hate it when you say that. All right, we will talk.*

"It's a possibility," Katie said, looking up at Calvin. "It sounds like the answer is positive. It just depends on what is required of me in return."

"You have to do things for them in return?" Calvin asked.

She looked around before answering. "For mine you do. She's pretty fucking smart."

"Why does it not surprise me that yours is a female?" Calvin chuckled.

What does that mean? Pandora growled. *So help me, I will come out of this body and—*

Katie chuckled. *Calm down, Women's Lib. Sheesh, he just meant because I'm such a force to be reckoned with. I thought you said feminism was stupid?*

Stow it and feed me another donut, Pandora snapped.

Katie rolled her eyes and bit into another donut, feeling Pandora's satisfaction roll through her. She didn't mind making her happy occasionally.

At least she got to eat whatever she wanted.

"So what will she ask for in return?" Calvin asked.

"Who freaking knows?" Katie laughed and wiped crumbs off her face. "It has been anything from quality time watching soap operas to unique clothing in the past, but I put nothing past her. I have to make sure that whatever it is, it doesn't *literally* bite me on the ass."

MICHAEL TODD

"Holy hell." Calvin's eyes widened. "I sure hope my demon just chills."

"They are demons, so what do you expect?" Katie chuckled. "She's smart to negotiate, that's for sure."

"Does she have anything to say about the demon that tried to eat my body?" Calvin asked. "Oh wait, the one that said he didn't like dark meat. He was just going to smash my body into a bloody pulp."

Tell him to stop with his whining already. He's alive, right? Pandora gruffed.

Try to understand that people of color have lived on this planet just as long—if not longer—than all others, and we have treated them terribly, Katie told her. *Oppression, slavery, killings, beatings, shame, and everything in between.*

There's a little bit of the devil in everyone, and besides, their own people did some of that too. Pandora snickered. *But that sucks, Calvin seems like an okay human—one I wouldn't make suffer before twisting his neck and popping off his head.*

Katie paused for a moment. *I think I should take that as a compliment?*

For him, yes, Pandora agreed. *I'd torture the fuck out of you, though. Hand you over to an incubus to loosen you the hell up.*

"She said he's powerful, three levels below the Seventy-Two," Katie said. "That because I took the knives from his skull he went back to hell, and can come back any time that he wants to. We have to trap and kill him here, or he will retreat next time as well."

"And the special metal we have helps with that," Calvin said, shaking his head. "It's all kind of working out perfectly, don't you think?"

"That's what I was thinking." Katie looked around them. "Where do you think the person that did this is from?"

Calvin pursed his lips. "Personally I think he or she is from Los Angeles, and came down here so this wouldn't happen in their backyard. Makes it harder to get caught in a different zip code."

"Why not Orange County?" Katie said. "There is plenty of rich, bored people there, and not a lot of suspicion."

"Because Los Angeles folks tend to hate the shit out of San Diego." Calvin chuckled. "It's the place with all the richies. It's where the celebs go to vacation while they complain about their own city. Los Angeles has worse crime and gets less funding per capita, and they loathe the people of San Diego for it. It's always been a feud. Besides, most of the places outside of a few rebuilt areas were constructed in the old days. There is an up-and-coming group of people there, but a lot of the older generation still lingers."

"This is insane." Katie laughed. "Even in the demon war they pick and choose what city they want to destroy first. Even demons have human tendencies."

"Or the human had demon tendencies." Calvin raised an eyebrow.

"My demon did say there was a little demon in every human," Katie admitted.

"I don't doubt that at all." Calvin watched her reach for another donut. "Some more than others, but I definitely have seen my fair share of assholes."

"Amen." Katie picked up another donut, licking the frosting off her lips.

"You need to get a handle on that," Calvin told her

"Mmmhmm," Katie moaned. "I will, just as soon as I'm done with this jelly one."

Calvin just smirked and shook his head.

When Korbin's meeting was over and he had exhausted pretty much his last lie to the people on the phone, he hung up and leaned back in his chair, groaning loudly.

He didn't need this kind of bullshit in his life at this moment. What he needed was for everyone to understand he was chasing demons, not playing politics.

He needed a damn breather, was what he needed.

He got up and went outside, taking a deep breath of the warm desert air. He looked at the other building and walked over, shoving his hands in his pockets. He went inside and through the outer area to the working level.

Korbin winced; the noise level was almost unbearable in here. Joshua was on the other side, working diligently with headphones on his ears. There was a shitload of big-ass machinery, and loud noises coming from the forge. The forge itself was fairly large. You definitely couldn't miss it, given the flames constantly shooting from it.

He shook his head and walked around some more to check out the space. When he heard heels tapping on the concrete behind him, he turned to see Mamacita walking toward him. He was surprised by just how attractive she was in her business suit, hair perfectly styled and heels that looked more business, less stripper-pole.

He swallowed hard and remembered that he was the boss, not some young kid coming to call. He nodded professionally at her and turned back around, clasping his hands awkwardly in front of him. He realized then that she had been the woman walking into the building earlier, so different in appearance he hadn't recognized her.

"To what do we owe the pleasure today?" Mamacita smiled. "I saw you outside earlier, but you looked preoccupied."

"Yeah." He pursed his lips. "I have a lot going on, and a lot of pressure mounting on my shoulders. Right now? Well, right now I am trying to figure out how to either make this place look like something it isn't, or move all this equipment again. The last thing I want to do is have another moving day, so let's just say that is Plan B—about a mile and a half below Plan A."

"Yes, personally I am not too fond of moving everything either, and Joshua would be upset to have to uproot right in the middle of his research and projects." Mamacita glanced at him. "He is a strange boy, but we love him."

"This is such a simple space, but loud. I would have to keep people from even coming through those doors," Korbin said, shaking his head.

"Well, that is easy," Mamacita said. "In order to do that, you must make it look like something everyone expects and understands. You don't want them to question, or even want to question, what is going on in here for two seconds. You want them to know deep down that it is exactly what they think it is."

"Like what?" Korbin wondered, furrowing his brow.

"What do you see here?" Mamacita asked, looking around the space. "What do you *physically* see in here?"

"I see concrete walls and a forge and lots of machines."

MICHAEL TODD

"*Ayi*," Mamacita exclaimed, shaking her head and rolling her eyes. "You are a practical and highly unimaginative man. Look beyond what you *know* you see. Tell me about the people."

"Well there is Joshua, who is young, several twenty-something women, and a couple who look like teenagers," Korbin said. "They are all modestly dressed for a working atmosphere, and they all look happy; at ease in their jobs. They look like they belong here in some way or another. I don't know what you want me to see. I mean, there is so much here that is just normal everyday stuff. Nothing looks odd or strange to me, but to a government official? Well, it would seem more than strange."

"Let me tell you a little secret," Mamacita said. "Those teens—they are Katherine's kids. They were born into the system, because we were not working as we should. They have to work, go to school, or do chores, or they don't get to play Xbox later. They know the rules."

"Katherine's kids," Korbin said, scrunching his forehead together again. "Holy shit, you are telling me I'm looking at a bunch of prostitutes?"

"Yep." Mamacita chuckled.

"And you think that the best way to cover this place is by making it look like a whorehouse?" Korbin said, looking at her in shock.

"Not just make it look like one, actually make it one." She laughed. "Though I do have to say you get points for not thinking of that first. You are more of a man than most. I will also throw in some points for you being so dense you didn't get it at first, but I can't decide if that is endearing or not. I know that with the job you hold, you don't look around you very often. If it is not trying to eat you or kill someone else you pay it no attention whatsoever, but the world—the rest of us—we are still out here, watching and doing our thing."

"Your *thing* isn't right," he snapped in frustration. "These are young girls."

"Who have the choice to leave whenever they like," Mamacita retorted. "Who are encouraged to build themselves above the system. You know what's not right, Korbin?"

Korbin looked down at the fiery woman, knowing he had said the wrong thing. He had pushed her buttons, and part of him felt bad about it.

He was judging something he didn't understand.

"What's not right is a bunch of people taking on the challenge of fighting for the ignorant, who don't have a clue they are in danger," she told him.

"You know too much," Korbin growled, bothered by that fact. "Katie has told you too much."

"Katie hasn't told us anything." Mamacita sighed. "Look, the bugs know when to get out of the way, cause that's the only way we will live. Armani…he treated us like people, so we had to figure out who you were. Now, though, we know Damian and Katie, and eventually we'll know you. Joshua is just as innocent as the rest of us. We are not stupid, Korbin. Well, not all of us, anyway. Some of us know what is going on, but we can't fight others, except those who have been human all their lives. But we *can* move our house over here, and build a house around the forge. We can do our part to help."

Korbin shook his head. "I don't know…"

"It will take money, sure, but do you know any government official who will come into a whorehouse with so many eyes watching or videotaping them?" Mamacita smiled.

"Maybe you are right," Korbin allowed, "but Lord help me, I have no idea how I am going to explain this to Katie if I decide to make this happen."

"You explain it as you doing what is best for your team, and for humanity," Mamacita told him with a nod.

15

Katie stared out the window at the cars passing them on the 405. They were on their way to Los Angeles, and had almost reached LAX. This area was a lot different than San Diego. Everyone was in a hurry and looked angry, and the level of smog in the air was almost unbelievable. She was starting to see why the people in Los Angeles would hate the laid-back hippie atmosphere of San Diego so much. She could also see why you would choose to live in San Diego over LA in a heartbeat. Still, it was a beautiful city with skyscrapers looming in the distance and angel wings painted on so many different surfaces.

Oh my God! Pandora squealed.

What? Katie said, jumping slightly, her hand lingering on the butt of the gun. *What do you see?*

Sweet Satan, my dreams have come true, Pandora replied. *The sign has shown itself.*

What? What sign?

Katie looked out the window, ready to see a demon standing in the middle of the city. From Pandora's reaction, she assumed the thing would be larger than King Kong. However, as she looked toward the airport she relaxed into her seat, shaking her head. She saw a sign all right, but it was a donut the size of a house in the distance next to a sign for Randy's Donuts.

You are going to get someone shot, Katie told her. *And I'm telling you right now, I will not allow any more weight to work its way onto these hips.*

I promise there will be none on your hips, Pandora said.

I don't want fat! Katie growled.

Fine, Pandora huffed. *But you need more curves.*

No fucking way, Katie said angrily. *Muscle! I need muscle!*

Fine...muscle, then, Pandora grumped. *Just get me more fucking donuts!*

I'll see what I can do, Katie said with a smile, thinking she had finally gotten the upper hand.

"I don't understand," T'Chezz growled, swiping his arms across the table and knocking everything onto the floor. "This was foolproof! You are not as much of an idiot as the others. You were supposed to secure this thing for us!"

"It wasn't that simple," the demon said, rubbing his head. "The bitch stabbed me in the fucking head from six stories up!"

"So?" T'Chezz growled. "You are a demon. That shit is not supposed to injure you."

"These were different," the demon admitted. "These

blades, they were made of something I've never felt before. It's like they have holy weapons or something. It damages us. If she hadn't pulled those blades out, I would have died right there in that dimension. I wouldn't have returned, and you would have been out another goddamned demon."

"These weapons…" T'Chezz began, crumbling a stone in his hand. He didn't care in the least whether the other demon died. "They were made by the priest?"

"I don't know," the demon replied. "There was no priest there. Just a girl, and a mouthy black man."

"Did you even fight?" T'Chezz growled. "And the girl… could you sense her demon? Obviously she has one. No human has those powers." He pulled a piece of meat out of his mouth, looked at it, and tossed it to the side.

Lunch.

He pondered for a moment. "Maybe it was my sister, that annoying bitch."

"I don't know." The demon sighed. "I was fighting the black guy pretty much the whole time. I was so close to killing him, the fight started to leave his eyes in his exhaustion. Then, out of nowhere this bitch lands on my shoulders and plunges her fucking knives into my damned skull. The pain was unreal, unlike anything I have felt before. My eyes blurred and my head was throbbing. There was no time to sense what demon she had in her."

"You still owe me," T'Chezz growled, turning around and staring at the demon. "I got you to Earth, but you failed to deliver the results I contracted for."

"Your human vessels are weak," the demon argued, annoyed. "I was set up to fail from the beginning, and you didn't mention any hellrats coming after me. I was prepared for those measly police, but got Robobitch and Eddie Murphy telling dick jokes while trying to kill me in the streets."

"Our contract is still in force," T'Chezz growled.

"I know," he groaned. "I fucking *know*. Obviously I will go back, but I want to wait. I want to catch them when they are not expecting it. They will be on high alert now, just waiting for me."

"No," T'Chezz yelled. "You will go back now; as soon as it can be arranged. There is no more time for tiptoeing around these humans. We are stronger and smarter than them. We can't allow these types of challenges to stand in our way while they celebrate their victories and pound each other on their backs."

T'Chezz slammed his fist on the table and walked out of the room, leaving the demon on his own.

He turned and looked out the window at the flowing lava in the distance, his lip curling into a snarl. He didn't like being pushed around, but he had signed a contract in blood. "Maybe T'Chezz should go to Earth and get stabbed," he grumbled. "Then we'll see how enthusiastic he is to go back."

The reporter was on her sixth house. "Did you see anything strange the other night?" Charlotte asked as a woman as she stood on her front porch.

"No," she said angrily. "I done told the cops to leave me at peace. I don't know nothing."

With that the woman slammed the door in Charlotte's face.

Charlotte took a deep breath and turned around, walking down the steps and back out to the curb. She put her pen back into the spine of her notebook and looked at the drug house on the corner. She knew someone had to have seen something. The place was right out there for everyone to see.

"I saw a car arrive," a voice said from beside her.

"You did?" she asked, pulling out the notebook again and smiling at an old man. The man had torn clothes and bad teeth, and the smell of whiskey emanated from his pores. He had stopped on the sidewalk with his cart in front of him.

"Oh yeah, fancy thing." He nodded. "Blacked-out Mercedes, I believe. It had some sort of special tag, but I couldn't see what it was. There was a driver in the front, and he let the person in the back out. I turned away at that point. I didn't want to be part of nothing like that. I knew something bad was going to happen."

"Right." Charlotte smiled, pulling a five from her pocket and handing it to the man. "Thanks a lot."

"Sure, sure," he said, turning back to his cart and moving down the street.

Charlotte was trying to remember that car. She knew she had seen it somewhere before. There had to be some sort of record of it coming to the neighborhood.

She headed toward the small businesses on the streets. She figured maybe someone in those shops had cameras that pointed in the direction of the house. She was hoping to get a good picture of the person who got out of that car.

With money like that in an area like she was in, they would have been someone important.

She stood in front of the house and looked up and down the street. The house cattycorner to the drug house had a camera mounted at the front door, pointed outward. She shook her head and walked over, knocking on the door.

"Yes?" The woman answered the door in a housecoat and slippers.

She looked up. "Hi, I'm Charlotte. I'm a reporter, and I was wondering… This camera up here, does it work?"

"Oh, yes," the woman told her. "I order a lot of packages from Amazon, and those little sonsabitches around here like to come by and snag my packages right off my front porch. Now if they do I can see exactly who did it, and either call their mama, 'cause usually they punk-ass little kids, or call the cops if I need to. I's recovered four different packages because of it, and now they don't come up on my porch so much."

Charlotte smiled. "That's a very smart idea."

"The only thing that's annoyin' is that it turns on any time it catches movement." She shook her head. "A car, a cat, a squirrel—anything sets it off."

"That stinks for you, but that's actually perfect for what I am looking for." Charlotte took a deep breath. "Is there any way you would let me see the footage from the other night, when the deaths occurred at the house across from you?"

"Oh, I didn't even think of that." She slowly nodded to herself. "Sure, sure, come on in."

"Awesome," she exclaimed, looking behind her as she entered the house and shut the door.

About twenty minutes later Charlotte emerged from the house once again, her disappointment reinforced. She couldn't seem to catch a break. It was almost as if the person had scouted the street beforehand. The camera had gotten a shot of the car, and a clear one at that, but the windows were blacked out and it was from the side. She couldn't see the tag, and the footage stopped at the hood of the car, so she wasn't able to see any faces either. The driver had a dark shadow over him as he got out and went around.

"I'm sorry I wasn't been any more help," the woman said.

"Oh, no." Charlotte smiled. "You were a huge help, thank you so much for your time."

"You're welcome. Be safe out here, a young thing like you." She shook her head. "It'll get dark soon, and you don't want to be on these streets by yourself then."

"Yes, ma'am. I only have a couple more things to do, then I'll be on my way." Charlotte smiled as she walked down the porch stairs and back to the sidewalk.

She sighed and shoved her folded notebook into the back pocket of her pants. She started walking, not sure where she was going but figuring maybe something would catch her eye. About a block down, she stopped and stared at a pawn shop located right there on the corner. They had cameras everywhere, every single one of which was pointed in a different direction—including straight down the street toward the drug house.

Charlotte knew the owners of the pawn shop wouldn't

be too keen on letting her walk in there and grab footage from their cameras. It was a bad neighborhood, and if they thought they could be implicated in getting some thug caught, they would stay far away. She thought about calling the police to get the information for her, but in this kind of neighborhood the owners would just say the cameras weren't working.

They wouldn't want any kind of retaliation against the shop, since it was their livelihood and a good one for an area like that. She looked through her bag and stared down at the camera inside. It was her most prized possession; she had worked for over a year to save up enough money to afford the thing. It was the reason she got so many cover stories for the publication—she had the camera there to point and shoot. She didn't make enough to pay a photographer, so that was pretty much her only move.

She knew she would have to use it to negotiate if she wanted to see that data.

She pulled out her phone, and looked through her received calls until she found the one from Calvin. If they wanted information they were going to have to help her get it, and that meant making sure she got her camera back after her effort. She wanted to know about her aunt, but this camera was the key to her livelihood.

Katie answered, "Hello?"

"Katie, it's Charlotte," she replied.

"Hey! Have you found anything out?"

"Just the color and make of the car," Charlotte said. "But look, there is a pawn shop here on the corner with cameras pointing straight at the drug house. I know that whatever they have on tape, it's going to give me something really good to go from. The thing is, they aren't just going to hand it over. I'm going to need you to promise me that you will get my camera out of hock when you are done."

"Your camera?" Katie asked, confused.

"It's all I have to barter with," Charlotte explained. "And it's the only thing I have to my name, so I need it back."

"All right," Katie agreed. "Write down the name and address of the shop and whatever I need to get camera back, and I'll take care of it. When you get the information, call us immediately."

"Will do," Charlotte said, pressing End.

She looked at the store and straightened her shirt, slightly nervous. She worked for a publication where you didn't go undercover very often. In most cases you were right out there in the open. "Undercover" to her meant finding the right bush to hide in, then pretending to be someone else.

She pulled out her camera and looked down at it sadly, even rubbing her thumb over the top like she was petting a dog.

"Don't worry, little camera," she whispered. "I'll make sure you get back home safe and sound, but first I gotta help find a world-class asshole."

Charlotte put on a tough face and put the camera back in her bag, then walked into the pawn shop. The owner came over from one side of his counter to the area closer to her and smiled as she approached the counter. He knew she was there for more than jewelry or DVD's.

"What can I do for you?" he asked.

"I need to see your camera footage from the other night," she told him.

"Do you have a warrant?" he asked, guarded.

"Oh, no. I'm not a cop, I'm a reporter." She smiled sweetly.

"Oh." He chuckled, then straightened his face and leaned across the counter, his hands clasped in front of him. "Then what do you have to offer me in return?"

Charlotte sighed and reached into her bag, slowly pulling out the camera and setting it on the counter. She was starting to think demon hunting wasn't as glamorous as it looked to be.

Either way, though, she was in it—and there was no turning back.

16

"The death of those children was not only devastating, but it is something I and the rest of the politicians in this country should take full responsibility for, I believe," the politician lamented as he sat in his chair. "There is no excuse for a bus full of children being captured and injured—or killed, in several cases —without the hand of God himself coming down on them." His voice rose as one of his fingers stabbed the air above his head. "There should have been strategies employed *long* before this to keep our children safe. They are the future of this world. Those tiny hands and tiny feet will sculpt our future." He dropped his arm and sighed heavily, weariness in his voice. "Now we have a bus full of children, including three whose families we pray for nightly, with terrible memories. From what I've been told they are all seeing therapists, but there is no excuse for a child to ever have to go through something that damaging —not when we could have avoided it from the beginning."

"And what are your plans to prevent future events like this?" an Hispanic male reporter asked.

The politician nodded and sat up a little straighter. "I am currently pushing legislation through that will make it a requirement for all buses to have tracking devices active at all times—paid for by the federal government of course," he explained. "We understand that the smaller communities don't have the funds to accomplish this, but their children are no less important than the ones who live and go to school in the larger communities."

"Well, sir, I have to say I am incredibly impressed by your demeanor and thoughts on the whole process," the reporter said, putting his notes in his briefcase. "Thank you for taking time from your busy schedule for us."

"Absolutely." The politician smiled, watching as the reporter stood up and walked out of the room.

As soon as he was out and the doors were shut, his smile faded. He pulled at his necktie, shaking his head. The driver, who also happened to be his righthand man, made his way to his boss and handed him a bottle of water.

"That went well." He chuckled.

He opened the water with a twist and took a swallow. "I hate fucking reporters," the politician growled. "But as it happens, I have a silent interest in the companies that will be bidding on this project if it goes through, so I'll make out on the end."

"What happens if you lose, sir?"

"I don't give a fuck." He shrugged. "I threw the dogs a bone. If I lose the bone, no skin off my back, right?"

"Absolutely." His driver laughed.

"Things didn't go as they were supposed to," a voice inside the politician's head spat.

The politician doubled over and grabbed his head, groaning slightly as he slid off the chair and onto his knees. Sweat dripped copiously from his forehead onto the floor as he shook wildly. He groaned at the pain of T'Chezz coming through mentally. His human body had a very hard time making connections like this.

"T'Chezz." The politician spoke out loud. "What can I do for my prince?"

We will try this again, he snarled. *And if* he *fails, so do you.*

His failure was not my fault, The politician wiped at the blood dripping from his nose. *I did everything you asked me to.*

Do it again, T'Chezz shouted.

"Yes," he said aloud, with fear in his voice. "Right away."

Good, T'Chezz growled, and cut off the communication.

The politician screamed and fell onto his butt on the floor. His driver rushed over, grabbing him under the arms and lifting him into the chair. He kept his eyes closed and breathed deeply, waiting for the ringing to leave his ears. His driver patted the blood from under his nose and held out the water bottle. The politician opened his eyes and nodded at the driver, then took the water and sipped it.

"Where is the document?" the politician barked.

"Here, sir," the driver said, handing it over.

"We have to do an operation tonight," he said, snatching the sheet from the driver's hand and unfolding it. "I just have to find a suitable location to let loose a small nuclear demon."

"May I suggest Inglewood?" the driver suggested.

"Those bleeding-heart liberals could do with a little more bleeding."

"While I'm always happy to barbeque a few dozen Republicans, I suppose sometimes our people have to take one for the team," the politician said, leaning back and smiling. "I wouldn't be a man of the people if I was picky, would I now?"

"My apologies," the driver said, slightly nervous. "I didn't realize that you were a Democrat. I thought it was all for show, given the companies that you do business with. Of course, these days who can tell, in politics? We have a president who was a Democrat until he ran, and is now a staunch Republican. I never did understand politics. I think that's why I just stayed the muscle of the group."

"You are too softhearted for politics, my friend." The politician smiled. "And that's a good thing. The rest of us make deals with the devil, literally. No, I'm not really a Democrat, just on paper. Both those groups will kiss my ring right after I've shoved my hands up their asses."

The driver laughed along with the politician, not fully understanding what he meant.

"It's a shame we don't have any real Republican areas in Los Angeles." The politician sighed. "I could definitely sit back and sip a beer to the harmonious sounds of demons crunching on Republican leg bones and the underlying symphony of their screams. It definitely isn't like it used to be. Don't get me wrong—it's not that I love Democrats. I just hate Republicans more. I guess you could call me a moderate. As in, I moderate which one I hate more at any given moment."

The politician laughed loudly as he folded up the sheet

of paper and handed it back to the driver. He stood up and fixed his sweaty hair, wiping his hands on the towel the driver handed him and tossing it on the table in front of him. He had fire in his eyes, and he knew that no matter how much he wanted to be done with the whole mess, he had to live up to his end of the bargain. He would never get what had been promised if he didn't.

"Come on, we have a demon to open a door for," he said, walking off.

Katie leaned forward. "Hey, take this next exit. I want to check out that gun store on the signs. There were some self-loading ammunition pieces that I wanted to see, and I'm sure a place like that would have the information I am looking for."

"All right," Calvin agreed enthusiastically. "I like to see you curious about weapons."

When they pulled up, there was a sign on the door prohibiting the carrying of firearms in the establishment. Katie sighed and pulled off her vest, gently laying it in the back and running her hand over her knives. She didn't like leaving them anywhere they could be found, and she definitely didn't like walking around without a weapon. Calvin looked at her as he took his guns out and set them in their cases behind his seat. He could tell she was nervous about going in unarmed.

He chuckled. "Don't worry, it's a lot easier to *not* be carrying when everyone in there has a gun. If you need one, just take one of theirs—although I don't see us having any issues in this tiny bit of time. You will be fine. Just think of it as walking in like any normal person."

"I feel naked," she grumped. "This is not what I wanted to do—be unarmed in this city while we were here."

"You'll be fine," Calvin told her as he shut the car door.

The two walked into the shop, and immediately Katie was drawn to the first case. They had anything and everything that she would ever need to arm herself—minus her special weapons, of course. Calvin and Katie proceeded from case to case, oohing and aahing at everything they saw. There were Berettas, Grubers, and special barely legal sawed-off shotguns with holster hooks built in so you could carry it on your belt without a long leather case. On the wall was every kind of crossbow she could imagine.

You are the only girlie in here, Pandora cooed. *The others don't seem to be paying you any mind, though. Maybe those curves are essential after all.*

Shhh, Katie hissed. *I'm busy here.*

Katie glanced at the other five guys in the shop, but as Pandora had stated, they weren't paying her any attention at all. She liked the fact that she was like anyone else in there, but it seemed like Pandora had been hoping for more.

She couldn't take her anywhere without her making some snide comment about the men, not even into a gun store.

Well, fuck, Pandora groused. *I guess that really was a gun in his pocket and he wasn't excited to see me in the least.*

Katie ignored Pandora's constant bitching about her lack of sexual attention and continued shopping. It took everything in her not to purchase something, but she didn't have an ID, and knew there was no way she could get anything there without one. She was turning to talk to the guy behind the counter when the alarm connected to the front door's metal detectors sounded. Two young thugs raced into the building, their pistols drawn. Katie straightened up, lifted her eyebrows, and stared at them like they were idiots.

"Everyone needs to…needs to…" The perps stopped in their tracks and glanced at each other.

Katie leaned against the nearest case and looked at the guys in the store. All five of them had drawn their pistols and pointed them at the perps. She chuckled and looked at the guy behind the counter, who had a sawed-off pointing in their direction. Slowly the two thugs lowered their pistols and tossed them on the floor, put their hands behind their heads, and spread their legs. They knew they had lost before they had even gotten started.

"So much for not bringing in weapons," Katie whispered.

"No. You see, all five of those guys are cops." Calvin chuckled. "They are allowed to carry anywhere. This has to be the worst place that you could ever try and hold up."

Bwahahaahaha, Pandora roared. *Humans are so goddamned stupid! Of all the motherfucking places to try to rob, these two fucking morons walked straight into a gun shop full of cops. Bwahahahaha! They deserve to be shot. Seriously, natural selection was never more perfect than in this case.* There was a slight pause before she continued, *Where are the bangs? Fuck me, I wish I had popcorn… Oh, come on! Where the hell are the flying body parts? Well, shit. This just went PG-13.*

Katie shook her head and turned back to the counter,

waiting for the guy behind it to put away his gun. She smirked as he rolled his eyes and shook his head, placing his shotgun out of sight under the counter and turning to Katie.

She shook her head and laughed.

"What can I do for you today?" he asked. "Now that the morons are taken care of."

"I wanted to know what it would take to run my own ammunition with special metals, and no, I don't know the metal's specs," she began.

"Hmm," he replied, rubbing his chin. "Something like that would take a specialist, and you won't find one anywhere around Inglewood. Where do you live?"

"Las Vegas."

"Uhmmm. The closest one to here would be a place in Las Vegas. Let me get you their information. They will be able to answer your questions better than I would."

"Thank you." She smiled as he pulled out his book and wrote down the information on a piece of paper. "You all be safe out there. It must be a full moon."

"You too." Katie laughed, nodded at Calvin, and walked out of the store.

Katie watched as the cops pushed the handcuffed idiots into the back of a patrol car. As the man shut the door one of the perps looked at Katie and smirked, his eyes flashing red. She grabbed Calvin's arm, nodding at the perp. The two cops standing closest to them were whispering and looking at Katie.

"What?" she asked, turning around and staring at them.

"Sorry," one of them said. "Not trying to be rude."

"It's just that, well, we were wondering," the other cop

began in a nervous tone. "Are you guys the D Squad? You match the descriptions a couple of colleagues from San Diego gave us."

"Man," Katie snapped, shaking her head and looking at Calvin. "You can't keep someone's mouth shut to save your life."

"I knew that threat wouldn't work," Calvin growled.

"You know what?" Katie smirked. "I think this time it just might work out in our favor."

"What do you mean?" Calvin asked.

Katie nodded at the two cops and smiled, then wandered over to the cop car and looked through the window at the perps. The one with the flashing red eyes snarled and growled through the glass for a moment, then his face went straight. It was obvious that he could sense Pandora inside her, and, well, none of the demons wanted to fuck with her—not even a little bit. Katie tapped on the glass and waved her fingers, and looked at one of the cops.

"Do me a favor," she requested. "I want you to take this fool out of the car, but leave the other one inside."

"Are you sure?" he asked. "That perp is a little squirrelly. He tried to bite my partner when he put him in there."

She nodded. "I'm sure he did. Just stay behind my partner. I got your back."

"All right," the cop said, opening the door and grabbing the guy by the collar. "You didn't want to go in there, and now you don't want to come out. Now stay right-fucking-there like a good boy and talk to the nice lady."

"Hi there." Katie smirked, rubbing her hands together and flashing her eyes. "Let's have a little fun."

17

C *an you do it?* Katie asked Pandora. *Can you do it right here in the parking lot without me being tied down?*

I can get it out, Pandora assured her. *But killing it before it takes anyone else? Well, that's going to be a little messy, I won't fucking lie.*

Meh, a little mess never hurt anyone, she replied. *What do you need?*

I need you in a chair, and I need a trash can. A metal one, she instructed.

"All right, boys," Katie said, looking at the cops. "I need a chair and a metal trashcan, stat."

Calvin nodded and went to grab a metal folding chair from inside the store while one of the cops grabbed a metal trashcan from behind the building. Katie sat down in the chair and cracked her neck, then stretched her arms way out in front of her. She looked up at the cops, who had all started to circle around her.

She reached up and grabbed the perp, pulling his face down close to hers.

"How you feeling, buddy?" Her smile didn't make him feel any better at all.

"No!" He shook his head, sweating. "Please, *no*."

"Come on over here," she said, standing up and pointed downward. "And have a seat in this chair for me. This is gonna hurt a lot, I'm not gonna lie to ya."

"The rest of you need to spread out," Calvin said. "Keep a nice wide-open space here. You don't want to be close when she pulls that demon out—not unless you want to join our team. You will be able to see everything just fine from about five paces back farther than you already are. Okay?"

The cops talked amongst themselves, the whispers going in one of Katie's ears and out the other. At that moment she was in the zone, being pulled into and released from Pandora's control like a wave. She gripped the perp tightly, watching his eyes flash red like hers.

"My mistress," the guy's voice hissed, his head tilted downward. *"I didn't know it was you or I would have never come here. Please accept my most humble apologies. There wasn't anything else to do and we heard about San Diego, so we figured it was time to get some of our own—at least until the master returns."*

"Quiet, you fucking fool," Pandora barked in Katie's voice. *"I'm goddamned tired of having to fool with absolute MORONS like you. You are here for one reason and one only, but still, you can't help yourself. You go jumping around town, flashing guns to cops and getting yourself locked up. You are a DISGRACE to*

the demon race, and you make me want to vomit all the fuck over you. What is your name?"

The demon whimpered.

"What IS IT?" she screamed.

On the outside she looked and acted like Katie, but the voice that came from her mouth was different.

It was a mixture of both their voices, melodic in tone but monstrous and fear-inducing at the same time. The cops stood around watching silently, with the hair on their arms standing straight up in the air. It was like a possession, only there was something about it that made everyone stand still. The other cop returned from around back and stopped, his eyes growing big.

Slowly he walked forward and set the metal trash can down next to her.

Katie glanced at it, nervous. She wasn't fully aware of what was about to happen, but she knew she was already far enough in that she couldn't turn back.

There was a demon in that kid's body, one that was controlling him. It was her duty to try to save him by getting that demon the hell off this plane of existence, but she didn't want it to leave the kid and go into one of the cops. She knew the only way to avoid that was to follow Pandora's lead.

Make sure it is unable to move when it's in the trashcan, then light that motherfucker on fire, Pandora told Katie.

Right, Katie said, and turned to Calvin. "A lighter… I need a lighter, too. Not matches, a good solid reliable lighter."

"Right." Calvin nodded, looking at the cops. "Does anyone smoke?"

The cops shook their heads, their hands on their pistols but their eyes glued to Katie/Pandora. The demon whimpered louder, shaking in his human capsule.

He knew what was coming, but then maybe he should have thought about that before rolling up on that gun shop like a complete moron. Calvin ran into the store again and grabbed a lighter from the owner, jogging back out and sliding it into Katie's front pocket.

"Good to go." He nodded at her in assurance and stepped back with the others trying to keep them as far away from her as possible.

He didn't know what to expect, since he hadn't been there when Garrett had been exorcised. That was different, though. In that one, there hadn't been five vulnerable bodies standing around for that demon to jump into.

All right, bitch, hold onto your panties, Pandora said.

Katie held the kid firmly as Pandora reached through her, grabbing the demon from inside of him. She let the kid go as his body fell back into the chair, unconscious. Katie's eyes grew wider when she focused on the demon hanging in the air in front of her, Pandora's gnarled claws holding tightly to its flesh.

This motherfucker is heavy, Pandora snarled. *Why can't they just come easy?*

Too many donuts? Katie asked.

Keep going. Pandora snickered. *I'll let him come in here with me.*

No, the demon growled, with fear in its eyes.

Everyone stood silently as the demon's body began to solidify. His skin cracked and tore as the spirit part of him morphed into a solid being. Katie'd had no idea that could happen, and judging by the surprise emanating from Pandora, it wasn't quite what she had been thinking either.

All right, on the count of three, grab him and shove him in that trash can. I can't keep my arms outside your body for long. Ready? One, two, three!

Katie reached forward without another thought and grabbed the demon, flipping it over and slamming it head-first into the trashcan, which vibrated from the demon's flailing. She stood steadily as Pandora pulled herself back inside, then looked up at Calvin for a moment and grimaced while she reached in and twisted as hard as she could to break the beast's neck.

"Usually he would heal before we could do this," Katie said calmly as she reached into her pocket to pull out the lighter. "But not on my watch. Never again."

She nodded at the high-quality Zippo, which had an Angel holding a skull on the side, then flicked it open and held it over the trashcan. After she'd lit it, she let it slide from her fingers and drop straight into the trash can as she stepped back.

Flames shot into the air, and everyone looked up as the first burst easily topped the store's roof. Katie leaned back and brushed her hands on her pants as the demon screamed and roared in pain.

She stood there until all was silent, then nodded in approval.

That, Pandora commented, wi*ll leave a serious fucking mark. He won't be able to come back for a decade, at least.*

Good. Katie smirked.

She turned to walk to the SUV, and the wide-eyed cops backed away to clear a space for her.

All of them turned to Calvin and nodded before taking the unconscious kid into custody again.

Katie couldn't help but notice how none of them would look her in the eye, much less allow themselves to be within two feet of her.

She climbed into the passenger side of the SUV and sat there staring at the flames shooting from the trashcan, not realizing that she had scared the living piss out of the cops.

That hadn't been her intention, nor did she like feeling as if she had pushed everyone out of their comfort zone.

Calvin grinned as he slid into the driver's seat of the SUV. "That was kickass."

Thanks. Pandora sighed. *All in a day's work.*

"That was terrible," Katie growled, turning to Calvin.

"What?" he asked. He had been about to turn on the car, but stopped.

What? Pandora snapped.

"Did you see the way those cops looked at me?" Katie ignored Pandora and spoke to Calvin. "They were fucking *terrified* of me, Calvin. They looked at you like they pitied you for having to be in the same car as me. None of them cheered or congratulated me, or even shook my damned hand. They were absolutely, completely, and totally scared out of their fucking minds by me."

"It's not *of* you," Calvin told her in a comforting tone. "Katie, you have to understand that most or all of them thought that D Squad was some made-up bullshit thing. They didn't believe the rumors were true. They were shocked, like every other human is when they see their first demon. They heard two people in your voice, and saw claws coming out of you. It was a little shocking, even for me, but they will come around—you'll see. They won't be scared of you for long. Soon enough they will be begging you to show up and help them."

"Still, it sucks," Katie said, a tear in her eye and her voice soft. "I felt like a circus freak."

Welllll, Pandora said in a high-pitched voice.

Shut up, Katie barked.

"Awe, come here." He leaned over and opened his arms. "Bring it in."

He wrapped his arms around Katie and she leaned her head against his shoulder, feeling the comfort. It had been a long time since anyone had hugged her, and that was exactly what she needed—a hug from her family. Calvin had become someone she could trust; someone who was there even when shit got really fucking weird.

"I'm serious, though," Calvin whispered into her ear. "That was like super-badass."

Damned right it was bad-ass. Listen to the black man preach the truth.

"Then you dropped that little bitch of a demon in the trash can and SNAP—you broke its fucking neck. Not to mention the damn flaming barrel! It was like some badass scene from a fantasy movie. I was so jealous it wasn't my black ass up there being all killer and shit."

Katie laughed through her tears. "I don't want to be a killer."

"Meh, there are worse things." Calvin chuckled.

I can think of something way better than being a killer, Pandora replied. *Being the bottom half of a black man sandwich, minus the filling—just two pieces of bread.*

Oh, God. Katie sighed.

Seriously, I have heard the rumors, Pandora insisted. *That the size of a black man's pecker is well above average. You should think about that for a second. Your mind might change after this embrace. Huh? Huh? No? How about now?*

Katie sat there for a minute still hugging Calvin, having to listen while Pandora went on about black men's dicks.

Finally she couldn't take it anymore, and started to giggle. She realized in that moment that this was her life, like it or not. The pity party had to stop.

What did she care about a bunch of LA cops anyway? Their stories would make her legendary, and she was on her way to figuring out how to solve this demon problem.

"What are you laughing at?" Calvin smiled as he pulled back and looked her in the eyes.

"Nothing," she said, blushing as she reached up to wipe off her tears.

"Whatever." He chuckled. "Tell me."

"Pandora—as I call her—my demon, she is...let's just say, *super*-sexual." Katie smiled.

Uh, no, Pandora spoke as if she were carefully explaining life to a young child. *I am normal-sexual. You are a damn prude who thinks that one dirty thought makes you a whore, and may the lord forbid you laugh at a dick question— especially when the answer might be sitting right next to your nun-ass.*

"What is she saying?" he asked with a smirk.

"She is making comments about black men and their size," Katie said, holding her hands apart as if measuring. "She has heard the rumors, apparently."

"Ah." Calvin laughed as he started the SUV and pulled

into traffic. "Well, Pandora." He looked at Katie, "She can hear me, right?"

Katie nodded.

"Well, let me start by saying that those rumors, no matter how fabulously true they are, are mostly good marketing by black men."

No! Pandora exclaimed. *It can't be true!*

"In reality only about ninety-eight percent of black men are truly huge," he continued as he turned left on a nearby street, having to speed between a Land Rover and a Mercedes. "The rest are normal, I assure you."

Okay, okay. Pandora came back down from her fear. *I have got to get this straight in my head. I need to do some serious research here. I'm not kidding. This needs to be done stat.*

Oh, lord. Katie put a hand over her eyes.

I need to start a bucket list of items, and "find out if Calvin is lying" is at the top, Pandora declared. *If he is telling the truth, this changes everything—my whole outlook on men. We are going to need volunteers; many, many volunteers. There are plenty of black men in Las Vegas, right? Hell, we should start while we are here in Los Angeles, I've seen one black man already! LOOK!* Katie's head twisted to the right just a bit. *There is one right there!*

You need to calm the hell down, Katie replied. *Leave my head alone. You won't be making a bucket list, and I am not going to start sleeping with a plethora of black men—or any men, to be specific about that. There is this wonderful thing out there called the Internet, where I can safely and without risk of pregnancy or STD find out anything you need to know about the size or shape or whatever.*

That's bullshit, Pandora grumped. *And how do you expect*

me to look on the damn Internet, you crazy non-ho-bag? I have no arms!

Lord, Katie moaned. *I owe you one, and will do the research with you on the internet, but we are deleting our browser history afterward. I don't need to get killed by a demon and have that pop up on my computer when someone goes to clear my things.*

I think that would be the best tribute to you, actually. Pandora giggled. *A musical montage of your dick size search results. It would be very exciting, and you wouldn't be there for the embarrassment. I would purposely possess someone just so I could see the look on everyone's faces when the schlongs appear on the screen. Oooh, maybe we can do it in one of those Imax theatres so there are dicks all around us. This is the best plan ever.*

I don't even know what to do with you anymore, Katie replied.

18

The night was dark. The sky was covered in clouds and rain was pouring down. Thunder roared in the distance.

Katie and Calvin had decided to stop for the night and rest up at a nice hotel in the city. When they had checked in, Katie was glad to get out of the public's eye. She smiled at Calvin and disappeared into her room, where happily she found a large jacuzzi tub.

She called down to the front and had them bring up bubbles and salts for a bath. It had been a long time since she had just relaxed and taken care of herself. House-keeping arrived at the door carrying a large basket of bath goodies, including candles and lotions. Katie smiled at them and passed the girl a tip before shutting the door and prancing to the bathroom.

Oh, goodie, Pandora exclaimed excitedly. *Pampering! I love pampering.*

I will only do it if you stay quiet and let me have some peace,

Katie snapped.

Yeah, yeah. Pandora blew a raspberry. *I was about to tell you the same thing. Always talking, never shutting up.*

Katie smiled and shook her head as she walked into the bathroom and set up the candles around the edge of the tub. She started the water and poured the salts and bubble stuff in, taking in a deep breath of the sweet lavender smell that filled the bathroom. She lit the candles and slipped out of her clothes, stepping and sitting down. She sighed as she scooted down in the tub, feeling the hot water completely cover her. She wanted it so badly—the relaxation—but every time she closed her eyes she saw the demon's face as it clung to her in fear, Pandora's arms stretching from her chest.

I'll take care of that, Pandora said when Katie sighed and tensed.

Thank you. Katie leaned her head back and closed her eyes.

She smiled as the face of the demon faded, and in its place a field of flowers appeared. She was running through them in a dress. She could almost feel the warm breeze blowing over her, and her eyes were bright blue in color. There was no red ring, no sign of the Damned, and she was free to explore whatever she wanted. Katie opened her eyes and looked up at the ceiling, realizing that daydreams were not what she needed. She'd had that life, and it would remain part of her. She needed to learn how to relax in *this* life instead of relying on her demon to take her to fictional far-off places.

My father told me about heaven when I was a young demon, Pandora told her. *He described it like the vision I just showed you. He couldn't understand why I wanted to go there. Of course, now I don't understand myself.*

Because you are not all bad, Katie said, breathing deeply. *Because somewhere deep inside you, you know what you are doing is right.*

Nah, Pandora said after a few moments of silence. *I just don't like flowers. Don't be mistaken, Katie...I am a demon, and I have fought beside my brothers to ensure the demise of humans. When this is all said and done and I have long left your body, I will most likely do it again and again, until your existence is only a whisper in the wind.*

Yeah, well, for now you are my ally. Katie sighed. *We will face that shit when the time comes.*

That's right, Pandora agreed. *And until then it's all about dicks. Lots and lots of dicks everywhere—all around me.*

Katie chuckled, waving her hand through the bubbles. *No. It's about righting wrongs and fixing this situation with your brother.*

Yeah, that too, Pandora huffed. *But mostly dicks.*

Katie sighed again. *You are a pain in my ass.*

Careful with your *words.* Pandora chuckled. *I could* literally *be a pain in your ass.*

Yeah, no. I really don't want that, Katie replied.

She laid there in the bathtub for about an hour, listening to the rain beat against the roof. They were on the top floor, and though she normally found that sound comforting, this time there was something about it that bothered her deep inside. She got out of the tub and dried off, then blew out the candles and stood in the darkness of the bathroom looking at herself in the mirror. She grabbed a robe and wrapped it around herself, then shook her head and walked out to the main room. The bed was welcoming, and she was asleep as soon as her head hit the pillow.

What seemed like only moments later but was around two thirty in the morning, Pandora woke in a panic. She shouted loudly, not knowing how to wake Katie from her sleep. She stirred slightly, but didn't wake up. Pandora started to play with her senses to rouse her, and Katie sat straight up in bed, gasping for air.

Sorry, Pandora began, *but shit is about to go down. Get up, put on some clothes, wake up Sir Long Schlong, and get ready to face that sonofabitch again.*

He's back?

I think so, Pandora admitted.

Katie grabbed her phone from the nightstand, and punched Calvin's speed dial.

"What's wrong?" he answered in a sleepy voice.

"There is a demon close by," she answered. "It might be the same one we faced in San Diego, so suit up good."

"All right," he replied. "Give me five minutes. I'll be over when I am ready."

Katie hit the End button and dropped her phone on the bed.

She got up and crossed the room to open her suitcase and pull out some clothes. She dressed quickly, grabbing socks and her boots and sitting down on the edge of the bed. As she laced her boots, she could sense Pandora trying to figure out where the demon was. It wasn't like her to be so helpful as to try and find the demon for her. She always stood back until the right time—the time Katie needed Pandora to be more powerful.

Why are you helping us? Katie asked.

Don't get your fetish panties in a twist. This bag full of dicks might know about my brother, Pandora replied. *I want to know as much as I can about his plans. I don't think you get it—he is a badass, even more so than me because he only sees death and destruction. He will cut your head clear off your shoulders and not think twice about it. He has no human emotions, nor will he be in a human body. When he comes, there will be more at stake than just your life. He'll take out, conservatively, everyone on the planet.*

Well, then let's kick this one's motherfucking ass and get some information out of him. Katie snickered. *I'm tired of being nice and trying to help everyone. I'm tired of being looked at like I'm a freak, so I figure, if they are going to look at me funny no matter what I do, I might as well go all-out. There is nothing more refreshing than just being my damn self.*

Preach it, girl. Preach it! her demon responded.

Calvin sat down on the bed and swallowed hard, thinking about the last time he faced this beast. It had taken something from him; something that he had yet to get back.

He felt like he had been turned into another person almost. His fear of death had been blown away in that moment, when he stood in front of the beast. In its place came the absolute certainty that he was about to die, and he was going to do it in a dirty San Diego alley.

Even after he no longer had to face that conviction because Katie had jumped down and plunged her knives into the demon's skull, his fear of death had never returned.

This was an uneasy feeling for Calvin, since he had stared several men in the eye throughout his life who had no longer feared death.

None of those men, however, had lived very long after that point. There was something sacred about that fear of dying; something that kept you wary of your actions, made you think about it very carefully before running into the fire.

It was something he feared he might not get back. He finished lacing up his boots and sat back for a second, gathering his composure.

He took his phone from his pocket and pulled up Korbin's number. He didn't look forward to waking him up, but they would need backup—or another team to come in when they were dead.

He didn't know what powers Katie possessed, but he knew exactly what their current problem child had, and her powers couldn't be enough to take care of that kind of demon.

"Hello?" Korbin answered, wide awake.

"And here I thought I was going to find you asleep." Calvin chuckled.

"There will be plenty of time to sleep when we are dead, Calvin," Korbin answered, stirring something in Calvin's chest. "So what's going on?"

"We are dressing to go out and check on a tip that shit might be going down," Calvin answered. "If true, a demon has arrived. It's large and angry—possibly the same one we met in San Diego."

"Lord." Korbin grunted. "All right, I am going to send Eric and Damian to Los Angeles immediately. They can be there in two hours, but I wish it were sooner. Try to stay out of battle until they get there, if possible. If the demon is in an unpopulated area, try to corral it until you have backup. I don't want them to find either of your dead bodies when they arrive."

"Will do, boss," Calvin agreed. "I can't promise anything, though. You know Katie."

Korbin chuckled. "Well, corral her too if necessary."

"Have them contact me when they land," Calvin requested. "I will let them know where we are, since at this point I have no fucking clue where we will find this thing."

"What's the source?" Korbin asked.

"I'm not sure," Calvin told him after a moment of silence. "Katie just woke me up. You can ask her when she is able to talk."

"Right." Korbin sighed. "Good luck."

Calvin nodded his head as if Korbin could see, pressed End. He shoved it back in his pocket and took a deep breath, looking at himself in the mirror. He pulled on his vest and shoved his knives into their slots, pumping himself up for battle.

There was a rap on his door. He walked over and opened it to find Katie waiting for him. "Here." She handed him a short sword. "It's made of our secret metal, and you're going to need it in this fight."

"Right." He accepted the sword. "Thank you."

She eyed him. "Are you ready?"

"I am," he answered. "Eric and Damian will be here in two hours to help."

"Let's hope we are still alive," she said, wiggling her eyebrows.

"Yeah." Calvin chuckled and grabbed the car keys.

Bring the donuts! Pandora screamed as Katie left the room.

Calvin and Katie took the back stairwell, knowing their outfits and weapons would surely be noticed in the fancy lobby of the hotel. They ran out the back and around, entering the parking garage and heading to the SUV. They hopped inside and looked at each other for a moment.

"Where are we going?" Calvin asked.

"I... I don't know," Katie admitted, turning inward. *Pandora, where are we going?*

Just drive, was the instruction. *Get on the 405 and drive south through the city. You will sense him.*

"Just drive," Katie repeated to Calvin. "Take the 405 south through the city. I will tell you when we are close to him."

"Can you trust her?"

"Yes," Katie said after a pause. "She doesn't want to go back to hell—not yet."

"All right." Calvin nodded. "If you trust her, I will too."

So, help me Pandora, if you are fucking tricking me I will make sure that another donut never crosses your lips, no matter how many centuries you live, Katie said.

I am not tricking you, the demon said calmly. *Just go.*

They headed out into the night, moving through the now-quiet streets and onto the highway. Katie rolled her window down and took in a deep breath, smelling the smoke from the fires on the hills. The wildfires were fully engaged, but these had been started by a person, not by an act of nature.

She sat back in her seat and let the rain mist her face as

the wind blew through the car. In the distance the sky lit up, bolts of lightning crisscrossing through it. It was an uncomfortable feeling, like nothing she had seen before, yet something inside her felt at home.

Katie didn't realize what it was about the scene that was familiar until Pandora spoke.

It's like hell is already here, Pandora told her as the fires raged in the distance. *Not even a fixer-upper at the moment. Those fires were started by humans. Angry ones—I can feel it. They weren't even Damned, just bad humans.*

A lot of good people live here too, Katie said. *A lot of people just working, going through life, raising families, caring for each other. However, it is a heavily populated city, and whenever you get enough people in one place, there are bound to be a few bad apples.*

You think that I don't know that? Pandora chuckled. *Never mind, there is no reason to explain. Just know that there was a reason we were released before, Katie.*

She didn't say anything else, not even a peep. There was an air of finality in her voice that cut to Katie's core and made her skin crawl.

She wasn't positive what her demon was trying to tell her, but it sounded like they had been released before to take care of the "bad apples" Pandora had just mentioned.

But who would release them?

From everything she knew, they could only be released by God himself. Why would God release such terror on people he claimed to love so dearly? She had seen the darkness in her soul before, but that night, under the striking lightning, she felt the darkness take another piece of her with it into the night.

19

Katie rolled up the window as the rain began to beat harder and sighed, looking around at the scene. It really was ominous, but she couldn't give in to the fear. There was a reason it was like that; a reason the night was now full of horrors. There was an awakening happening, an awakening that no human on Earth would survive if it weren't for people like her and Calvin.

They had to stand strong. To be there. To fight until they couldn't fight any longer, and with their last breaths, to continue to swing their swords until death found them.

The thoughts flew through Katie's head, but inside the car there was only silence. She could no longer feel that fear Calvin usually experienced before they walked into battle.

It was gone, as if it had never been. She didn't know if her senses had dulled or Calvin had reached a point in existence where he no longer feared death, but whatever had happened, the silence was deafening.

"Anything?" Calvin asked.

"Nothing yet." Katie sighed. "We just have to keep going."

"Right." Calvin nodded.

Calvin glanced out the window at the fires up on the mountain as he drove. They blazed wildly, lighting up the night sky and casting a red and yellow haze across the horizon.

He wondered if there were people there. People fighting those blazes, trying to save their homes, their city. He wondered what it was like for those people when they went home after a long shift to their family, beaten and bruised but nonetheless loved.

Something in him yearned for that, but he knew he would never have it. As they approached the large Randy's Donuts sign again, Katie looked up.

"Now! Here!" she called frantically, pointing to the side. "Take this exit. I can feel the demon!"

Calvin swerved off the 405, down the exit ramp and to the stop sign. He rolled his window down and listened for a moment. There were screams coming from the Inglewood Park Cemetery. Calvin turned to Katie, who looked that way with worry.

That's it, Pandora said. *Ahead in the cemetery.*

"She said he's ahead in the cemetery," Katie said.

"Man." Calvin shook his head. "Why do they always gotta be in the scariest fucking places imaginable? Like, pick a flower garden or something, for fuck's sake."

"But then where would we get our horror movie ideas?" Katie laughed. His comment had lightened the mood.

Calvin nodded. "All right, here goes nothing."

Calvin pressed the gas pedal and slowly sent the SUV toward the cemetery entrance. The massive bronzed gates were wide open, and one hung off its hinges. Katie leaned forward and stared out the front window as they got closer, frowning. There were so many damn people in the cemetery, and they were all running around screaming. Some were healthy, but others looked the worse for wear. Katie looked at Calvin.

"What the fuck are all of these people doing at a cemetery at three o'clock in the damn morning?" she asked. "Like, who goes for a lovely stroll through the cemetery at this time?"

"I have no damn clue," he said, shaking his head.

Calvin pulled off to the side and parked the SUV.

They climbed out and went around to the rear, opened the back door, and pulled out their gear for this op. Katie still wasn't sure what they would be facing, but it was obvious they wouldn't be alone.

She could hear dozens of sirens in the distance, and they were getting louder by the second.

That was exactly what she *didn't* want—a bunch of hot-headed cops swarming the scene, making things that much worse.

When it was only a couple of them they could handle it, but when there were dozens they couldn't protect all of them while trying to take down whatever demon was causing the issue.

"This isn't going to stay under the radar," Katie said, looking at Calvin.

"Not our fucking problem at the moment, missy!" Calvin grunted as he pulled out a heavy satchel. "That large motherfucker ahead of us is our goddamned problem right now."

Calvin pulled out the short sword that Katie had given him and held it up to the light. Katie stepped out from behind the truck and scanned the cemetery, tilting her head to the side. Standing even taller than last time was a very angry, very fiery demon. His eyes glowed bright red, and his hands and arms were swathed in flames. She took another step and her mouth fell open slightly.

Please tell me I am hallucinating, Katie begged. *Please tell me that giant motherfucking demon is not on fire right now.*

Appears so, Pandora chimed in. *Well, I wasn't expecting that. Apparently he has an affinity I wasn't aware of. Hmmm.*

Katie gawked. *You think?*

Well, there go the Molotov cocktails, Pandora joked. *No matter. We'll just drink the booze instead.*

Please tell me you didn't know you would be sending me into a fucking inferno with claws when you woke me up, Katie pleaded.

Uh... no, Pandora replied. *Human flesh doesn't usually hold up too well against fire. I'd really like to keep the skin on your body for right now.*

So would I. Katie sighed.

Just then shots were fired and Katie ducked, trying to figure out who was shooting. The cops hadn't pulled up yet, so it couldn't be them. It was LA, though, so just about anyone could have a gun. Finally she spotted a guy dressed in jeans and a wife beater with a red bandana around his head standing right in front of the beast, emptying his gun into his gut.

Trust LA to have gangbangers who aren't going to allow shit on their land without responding. Katie shook her head. *Courageous. Stupid, but courageous.*

I feel like "courageous" is way more than that idiot deserves, Pandora disagreed. *I feel like "stupid as fuck" and "too dumb to know better" are much better descriptions for him.*

"What the hell is that stupid motherfucker doing?" Calvin asked as he walked up. "He obviously has zero clue what he is working with here."

"I feel like I need to do something, but the scene is just so unreal," Katie remarked.

"Snap out of it, crazy. We need to get in there." Calvin chuckled and ran toward the demon.

She nodded and sprinted after Calvin, who was traveling straight toward the demon in the middle of the cemetery. There were crushed headstones all over the place, and in at least two different spots Katie couldn't tell what a random body part was. She took a deep breath and slowed down, following Calvin over to a hedge and bending down next to him.

"Okay, what's the plan?" Katie asked.

"Well, first we have to get numbnuts out of there before he becomes something sticky on the bottom of the demon's foot," Calvin said. "Then we attack, I guess. Try to keep him in the cemetery so he doesn't hurt anyone else."

"Any ideas about how to get the dumbass out of there?" Katie said, nodding her head toward the gangbanger.

"I don't know," he said. "It's obvious he can't hear us, but if we can get his attention we might be able to lure..."

Before he could finish his sentence the demon growled out loudly. He leaned over and picked the gangbanger up by the ankles, and dangled him upside down in front of him. Katie grabbed Calvin's shoulder hard but stayed down. She knew that running in there wasn't going to help anything. They watched as the beast sniffed him and growled, then repeatedly slammed him to the ground, sprays of blood hitting everything around him. Katie winced every time the body was lifted again. When the demon was done with that he raised the body and ripped the human's head off, throwing the rest of the body over his shoulder.

Calvin licked his lips "Well, I guess that means we can move on to Step Two now."

"Not if he gets out of this graveyard," Katie said, rushing forward. "And watch your step," she called over her shoulder. "There's pieces of that gangbanger everywhere."

Katie ran across the grass, jumping over broken headstones. Calvin yelled to stop her as she ran through the demon's legs and she froze, realizing that they had reached the edge of the cemetery. She didn't know what to do so she pulled out her pistols and shot straight up, striking the demon in the underbelly. Calvin let out a round with his gun as well, which struck the beast in the back of the head. They knew it wouldn't hurt him very much if at all, but they wanted him to walk back into the cemetery.

The demon shook its head and turned around to find where the bullets were coming from. Katie remained underfoot and out of his sight, while Calvin ran and hid so as not to provoke the demon any further. They weren't sure what their plan of attack would be, but they knew they had to come up with one soon or everyone was going to die.

As Katie turned to watch the demon stalk toward Calvin, her eyes fell on the multiple dead bodies of the street people who had initially attempted to fight the demon. Her heart felt heavy, but then she got angry.

"You see this, Pandora?" she snapped aloud. "These are *our* people. They might be down on their luck, or they might not have all their arrows in their quivers. They might even be brave to a fault, but no one fucks with us. We'll fight back, even if it means losing our lives. These demons, the ones like you, they think this will be simple— that we will just lie down and die—but they've got another think coming. Fuck with us at your peril, because we fucking bite back."

The two of them tried to keep the beast occupied, taking a few minutes to play "dodge the headstones" with the fiery abomination as he kept pulling them up and tossing the missiles at them. Others joined, so Katie and Calvin pulled back to their SUV to regroup for just a moment.

There were several civilians out there keeping the beast distracted, despite Katie and Calvin's warnings.

They grabbed their water bottles and stood at the back of the truck, breathing heavily and trying to figure out their next course of action. The cops were pulling up in rows, parking behind the black SUV and stepping out of their cars with wide eyes and shocked expressions. It took a couple of moments, but eventually they got their bearings and started to assist with getting the innocent bystanders out of harm's way.

Katie looked at Calvin and shook her head.

"This thing is huge," Katie commented. "It smashes everything it touches."

"I know," Calvin replied, "but we can't just stand by and let it destroy everything. We don't have enough time to wait for Eric and Damian—it's just not possible. We have to act soon; we can't wait much longer."

"All right," Katie said in resignation. "Then we are going to need a plan."

"Right." Calvin seemed slightly distracted.

"Calvin," Katie said. "You okay? I don't need you shorting out right now. I need you here with me."

"I'm here, Katie," he said, shaking his head. "I promise."

Pandora snickered. *Apparently* everyone *knows that.*

Katie turned and looked out at the sea of cops behind them. The ones next to them had their doors open, the radios blaring loudly. She could hear a familiar voice—one from the gun shop.

The radio crackled, then, "Be advised that there are two friendlies on the scene, a white woman in her twenties and her partner, a black male in his thirties. These two are vital to the survival of you and the people at that scene. They are special agents, so you are to leave them alone and let them do their job. Do not fuck with these two, especially the woman. Do not piss the woman off."

I wanted you to have appeal, but not the kind where men think you will eat them for supper. Pandora laughed.

This is your fault, Katie growled. *You have to be so showy about every damn thing you do.*

No, your job's just that dark, that's all. Pandora scoffed. *You can't have it both ways, Katie. You can't be a demon hunter, and have it be pretty roses and flowers.*

You don't think I don't know that? Katie snapped. *Now, if you would be so kind, please light a fire under Calvin's demon so that we can kick this beast's fucking ass and go the hell home.*

Pandora sighed, but said no more. She could tell that Katie had reached her breaking point, whether she wanted to admit it or not. There were a lot of things that could bring her to that point, but Pandora had never imagined it would be how other people thought of her.

At the same time, though, Katie had been surrounded by people like her—Damned—since she had made the change. It wasn't easy for humans when they felt disconnected; shunned, even.

She had never felt that way—and she wouldn't have given a rat's ass if she had—but she could feel what Katie was feeling. That was enough for her.

Katie walked over to Calvin and stared him straight in the eyes while putting her hand to his chest. He knew what she was about to do, so he just closed his eyes and nodded. Pandora took Katie's body for just a moment, pulling back her hand and slamming it hard against Calvin's chest. Calvin gasped, tightening his fists as his demon woke.

"Shake a leg and help your human," Pandora growled, Katie's voice intertwined with hers. "Or so help me I will make your life here on this plane a living hell."

"They need you," Korbin had told the guys before they left the compound.

Damian and Eric knew that what they were walking into was more than just a little incursion. It was the new wave of demon happenings, and they were in for a show—that was for damn sure. Korbin had seemed nervous, something he never was before a battle started, and it worried Damian. He was used to the calm and collected Korbin, even in times of strife and battle. He was used to the man who stood strong and laughed in the face of death, throwing himself in front of every bullet he could find. He was not, however, used to the Korbin who looked as if he were saying his last goodbyes. This new demonic wave had really pushed them all to their limits.

Eric drove the SUV to the airport, but the ride was silent. Damian wiped down his cross as Eric stared forward, driving quickly through the streets to the private jet entrance of the airport.

They took off, landing an hour or so later at LAX and slipping into the private jet area. When the stairs dropped Damian looked outside, unsure of what they were about to face. The plane had parked where it normally did, but instead of their sleek black SUV, there were at least half a dozen unmarked vehicles standing by.

"What is this?" Eric asked, undoing his seatbelt.

"I'm not sure, but let me talk." Damian stepped out of the plane.

"You must be Father Damian." A tall middle-aged man dressed in tactical gear was walking toward him with his hand out.

"It's better if I don't shake your hand," Damian warned him, eyes flashing. "We need to get going."

"We know," the man said. "I'm Sergeant Avery, and I will be airlifting you to the scene. We will brief you on the way."

"All right," Damian said, nodding back to Eric. "Can your men help us grab our gear?"

"Absolutely." The sergeant nodded, twirling a finger in the air. "People, round up!"

When they were securely in the choppers, Damian pulled out his phone and looked down at the screen. Every minute they weren't in the air was one more minute Calvin and Katie were fighting alone. He scrolled down to Korbin's number.

"Are you there?" Korbin asked.

"Almost." Damian gave the sergeant the thumbs-up from the back.

"We are getting the red carpet treatment from the Feds,"

he yelled. "They are airlifting us over. You might want to keep that jet close by."

"Right," Korbin said. "I'll have it come back and get it prepped and ready in case the rest of the team is needed. Thank you, Damian, and please look after them. We need our team back in one piece, especially with the changes in the air."

"Absolutely, boss," Damian assured him.

"And Damian?" Korbin replied. "Take care of yourself as well."

"Absolutely, sir," he agreed, hanging up the phone.

He looked out the window as the chopper rose high into the air and sped off toward the north. He wasn't sure what they would find when they got there, but he knew that if the Feds were picking them up it couldn't be good in the least.

He had to admit, he hadn't been fond of the idea of letting the Feds in on their secret, but in that moment it was definitely to their advantage. That chopper could get them there in a quarter of the time it would take the SUV in the shitty LA traffic, no matter how hard they pushed it.

He just hoped getting there sooner would be the key to winning.

The demon snarled and growled as he kicked over headstones and ripped trees from the ground, throwing them at spectators. He was growing tired of the games; growing tired of being targeted by the demon hunters and the human police. They had shot round after round at him, but still could not get it through their heads that the bullets didn't even pierce his skin.

What they *did* accomplish, however, was annoying the hell out of him.

He walked forward and kicked at one of the cops but missed, which made him stumble. As soon as his head tilted downward, the cops unleashed another round of bullets at him. He closed his eyes to protect them, since that was the only thing they could actually damage.

He snarled as he caught his balance, opening his eyes and looking angrily down at the ground. Slowly he raised his head, mouth dripping drool down his chin to his chest. He smirked as he leaned down and pulled a large tomb's sculpture from the ground. He gripped it tightly in his claws and pulled back in preparation for throwing, almost as if he were a pitcher on a baseball team.

Everyone froze in place for just a moment as they watched the mammoth beast lunge forward and release the stone carving.

It flew toward the crowd, striking two cops before it hit the ground. Dirt and blood blew into the air as the stone skidded across the ground like a rock on a pond. Several other cops dove out of the way before the statue crashed into the cop car.

"Whoo....whooo...who...w..." The cop car's siren whooped a few seconds longer before falling silent, the car lying smashed and broken on its side.

The creature laughed deeply, shaking the trees around it. The cops stood and dusted themselves off, dropping their arms to their sides in defeat.

The monster had won that round, and the cops were

beside themselves. They had unloaded an enormous amount of ammo on the demon, but all it had done was make it even angrier.

This looked and felt like a hopeless situation.

One by one the cops turned to look at Katie and Calvin, unsure what to do next. They were too close to a residential area to use heavier artillery, but they couldn't let the creature leave the grounds.

"You fools!" The demon laughed loudly. "You think your guns can stop me? The Reckoning is upon you, and the only thing you can do is surrender and hope for mercy from our leader."

"Fat chance," one of the cops yelled, spitting on the ground.

"Fine," the demon snarled. "Have it your way. Let's see how many children I can peel out of their beds."

The beast stretched its shoulders, its black flesh cracking and writhing on its shoulders.

Katie scrunched her face. "We can't let him leave, Calvin."

"Agreed," he replied, trying to figure out an angle—hell, *any* angle—to keep him around. "Ideas?"

She looked around for a moment, running her hands over her vest. Her palm stopped on her knife and she took a deep breath, pulled out the blade, and sprinted forward.

Pandora helped, increasing her speed and pushing her body. She spun between the beast's legs, slashing with her blade before running back to the side of the car.

The demon roared and grabbed at the gashes in his calves and ankles. Slowly he turned around, his eyes glowing red and anger oozing from every orifice.

It clasped its mighty claws together and roared again, blowing Katie's hair wildly around her face.

She smiled up at the beast and stood her ground.

"Stand and fight," she screamed, raising the knife in the air.

The demon laughed, throwing his head back and grabbing his stomach. When the laughter ceased he looked straight at her, Damned and demon brightening the night around them.

Slowly he lifted his hand and gave her the middle finger, turning to walk away once more.

I got this, Pandora told Katie, then, "*Convertam te, et vocavi te pugnare cadere*," Pandora hissed in Katie's voice.

The demon spun around with a look of recognition on its face.

What did you just say? Katie asked.

I called him a coward and told him to fight, Pandora replied in a shaky voice.

"T'Chezz *habet in capite pretium canis*," the demon roared. "*Quia videtur tam parvam caput est, ne hoc modo.*"

"I really need to brush up on my Latin," Katie whispered out loud. *What was that?*

He just said that T'Chezz has put a price on my head, and since it is such a small head he doesn't see why taking it is such a big deal, Pandora replied.

Katie sighed. *Oh. Sorry I asked.*

You are the one who wanted to practice like it was my brother, Pandora reminded her. *What better time than the present, right?*

Ehhhh, Katie groaned, sizing him up. *This was not what I had pictured.*

Not enough flowers and pink puffy things? Pandora asked.

If I could stab you without hurting myself I would do it right now, Katie told her dryly. *I just didn't realize the bastard would be so damn big. He came back bigger and fierier than before.*

They have a tendency to do that when you piss them off, Pandora replied. *I told ya, you should have never pulled those knives out.*

I got it the first time! Katie huffed.

Over to the side Calvin leaned against the SUV, catching his breath and reloading his weapons. The guns weren't doing anything at that point, but he knew that if they weakened him enough they would work. He had barely survived the heaving of stones, but his demon had woken up a bit and pulled him out of the way of two different trees. He didn't feel it was the right time to start a conversation with the thing, but at least he was taking notice of what was going on outside of his body.

Calvin finished loading his guns and put them back in his side holsters. He pulled his short sword from the sheath on his back and stared at the glimmering steel in front of him. He hadn't had a chance to use one of Katie's new weapons yet, but having the blade was definitely helping to get him pumped up and ready to take on the beast again.

He wanted to feel the power everyone else had felt when they were slicing and dicing their way through demon scum.

He found himself slightly disappointed that there were no smaller demons to take care of at that moment. He would rather have practiced before using the sword.

He shrugged and slid it back into its sheath.

As Calvin adjusted his vest's straps and readied himself

to get back out there the wind started to blow harder across the lawn, and it brought the sounds of the whirling of helicopter blades not too far away. He looked behind them, squinting his eyes as the dirt began to whiz around him. From below the hill a chopper rose, its guns pointed right at the beast and Eric and Damian looking down at Calvin. He chuckled and saluted the men.

Damian slowly lifted a small device with a red button at the top into the air. Calvin squinted, realizing that it was attached to the gun turret on the front of the helicopter. He nodded and quickly turned to his teammate.

"Katie!" he yelled. "Get down!"

Katie turned her head and saw the chopper, and she dove to the ground, covering her head. Immediately Damian pressed the button, unleashing round after round of high-velocity bullets into the demon. The shells fell to the ground below them as smoke billowed from the guns.

"Hot damn." Calvin laughed and clapped his hands.

The demon doubled over and put one hand on the ground, blood dripping from its chest onto the grass. It gurgled and growled as everyone remained still, waiting to see what would happen next. Katie slowly pulled her arms from over her head and turned over to stare up at the beast. She looked at the long claw embedded in the dirt beside her, and had just tilted her head to the side to get a better look at its face when its eyes shot open, glowing orange. He smiled and grabbed the tombstone under his palm, pushing himself to his feet and launching it hard and fast into the air.

Katie turned and screamed, reaching her hand futilely toward the helicopter to signal them to watch out. She could see the gleam of Damian's cross dangling around his neck. The headstone soared through the air directly at the helicopter, almost in slow motion. Katie dropped to her knees and covered her mouth.

"Nooooo!" she screamed.

Damian and Eric stared forward out the chopper window as it approached the cemetery. They could now see the demon, and were shocked at how huge the damn thing was. As they rose up above the hill Damian spied Calvin standing by the SUV looking up, and Katie standing directly in front of the beast, her knives in her hands, screaming something at it.

"Why am I not surprised?" Damian called.

"You ready?" the sergeant asked, handing Damian the remote control for the guns.

Damian laughed. "Oh, yeah."

He looked down at Calvin and held the device in the air, making a gun of his fingers and watching until understanding hit him. He put up his thumb and nodded, turning toward Katie. He couldn't hear him, but he knew Calvin was screaming at her.

She turned and looked up at Damian, a smile moving over her face. He watched in slow motion as she dove to the ground and covered her head.

He pressed the button, spraying bullets into the demon's chest, but he stopped when the beast doubled over in pain and fell to one knee. For a moment, time stood still.

Katie rolled over and looked up at the demon, tilting

her head to the side. Suddenly her face changed, and the demon slowly stood up, his eyes glistening in the very early morning sky.

The demon threw something that at first looked like just dirt, but as it spiraled toward them he realized it was a tombstone from the graves below them.

"Fuck," the sergeant yelled, turning the chopper to the left.

He wasn't fast enough and the stone struck the tail of the helicopter, knocking it completely off. The pilot grabbed the cyclic with both hands and grunted, trying to keep the bird upright. Damian grabbed onto the seat beneath him, closing his eyes and saying a quick prayer.

"Hold on, folks. This is gonna be a sucky landing!"

As the pilot struggled the helicopter tipped back and forth, backing away from the scene toward the road. The blades dipped sharply to the side, just barely missing the ground under them. Slowly the pilot took the chopper down. It spun in a circle before landing roughly on a clear plot of grass at the front of the cemetery, then tipped over. The blade dug deeply into the ground, which made the cockpit jump. Once the damned thing stopped moving, Damian blew out a deep breath and released his grasp on his cross.

They had made it through that. Now they had to just keep going.

21

Katie saw the stone hit the tail of the helicopter, taking it clean off. She put her hand over her mouth and gasped, staring as it wobbled back and forth, then spun in a circle. Calvin nodded to indicate that he would keep track of the demon, so she could take a moment to watch the crash.

As it dipped below the hill she stood up and ran forward, watching the helicopter blades dip dangerously close to the ground. However, right before impact, the pilot pulled the chopper up and landed hard in a grassy patch at the front of the cemetery before it tipped over. She was able to finally stop holding her breath when it looked like her teammates were safe.

Katie let out a deep breath and dropped her arms, feeling the anger starting to swell inside of her.

That was some good flyin', Pandora drawled in her best southern accent.

Katie slowly turned back toward the demon, who

growled at the chopper. She took off running toward it, stopping just short as it bent down and grabbed another stone, this one bigger than the last. She pulled her swords up as the demon reared back, ready to launch another attack on the chopper. She couldn't let him do it; those were her teammates struggling to get out of the helicopter, defenseless against the stone.

She screamed and took a step forward, but before she could go any farther shots hit the demon in the eye. Katie turned to Calvin and smiled as he walked forward, firing round after round into the demon's face.

"You know, I am liking this target practice on something so fucking huge." Calvin laughed, no fear in his face. "Though I must admit, if my target was his dick I would definitely miss. It's just so damn small. I mean seriously, I thought a beast like him would have a massive schlong, but nope! It's itty-bitty."

Katie turned back and watched as the beast swatted away the bullets like flies, growling loudly in Calvin's direction. She could see the frustration building on the demon's face, but she wasn't sure where to go at that point. Calvin just kept coming, blasting away, reloading, and blasting again. He knew the bullets wouldn't kill the creature, but he was trying his best to get the demon's attention off the helicopter long enough for them to evacuate.

"Move your asses, Damian," Calvin shouted over his shoulder. "I can't hold this thing off forever."

The demon looked at the chopper as the men pulled themselves free and ran in different directions. He snarled, lip quivering and saliva dripping from his sharp teeth. Katie could see the muscles in his black-scaled arm twitching as he shifted his body toward Calvin. Calvin knew it was coming, but he wasn't about to back off. Instead, he pulled his shotgun out and cocked it.

"Fuck you, motherfucker," he screamed, letting the shots fly. They struck the demon in the chest, but barely left a mark.

Calvin's eyes opened wider. "Well, *shit.*"

The demon reared back and flung his arm forward, releasing the stone in his hand. It missed Calvin and ricocheted off the tree in front of him. Calvin laughed loudly for a moment, but the stone had broken into large pieces when it impacted the tree and a rebound hit him squarely in the chest, knocking him backward onto the ground. Katie could hear the bones in his chest crunch as the stone made contact.

"NO," she screamed, running across the lawn toward Calvin.

She slid in next to him like she had made a home run and groaned, lifting the stone from his chest and throwing it to the side. For a moment he was still, not a sound coming from his motionless body. Katie grabbed his shoulders tightly and pulled him into her lap, tears beginning to flow down her cheeks.

"Come on, you stupid motherfucker," she whispered. "Don't leave me now. This is not the fucking time for this shit. I haven't shown Pandora the websites yet. You are supposed to be there to make fun of us, dammit! *WAKE. THE. FUCK. UP!*"

Katie pounded hard on his shoulders, which caused a deep wheeze to emerge from Calvin's chest. She gasped and lifted his torso. He opened his eyes and looked up at her, cracking a smile. He coughed and blood spewed from his mouth, covering his teeth. Katie shook her head and checked him over really fast. He was hurt, but the demon could help. She *knew* it could.

Maybe, Pandora said doubtfully. *He's not like me, Katie.*

Shut up, Katie growled. *Just talk to him.*

Put your hand on Calvin's chest, Pandora instructed.

Katie nodded at Calvin and put her hand gently on his chest. He winced slightly and she closed her eyes, unable to take the pain he was showing. Pandora took a deep breath and growled.

I told you to get to work, she snarled. *Now heal him the best you can, then get back out there. I promise you that if you don't pick up your slack, I'll make your death more painful than you could ever imagine. T'Chezz will have nothing on the torture I'll bring you.*

Katie gasped slightly when she felt the demon's power flow as he started healing Calvin as fast and well as he could. Pandora was right—he was not nearly as strong as she was, but that didn't stop him from pushing the bones back into place and mending them pretty well.

Katie sat there breathing heavily as Calvin twitched and groaned, imagining the pain and agony he was feeling with every movement of a bone.

She gritted her teeth and balled her fists, helping him through it and wishing that Korbin were there, or Garrett, or anyone who could help him right now.

In the background she could hear shots being fired, the demon growling, and general destruction, but she didn't care. Her focus was on Calvin.

When the demon stopped Katie sat up, staring at Calvin

and waiting for a sign. Slowly he opened his eyes and glanced at Katie, his face blank. He looked up at the sky.

"Fuuuck," he moaned. "That fucking *suuuucked*. But tell Pandora that she is one badass bitch for scaring the shit out of my demon. Never felt him move that fast or that panicked *ever*."

"I'll let her know." Katie chuckled.

Calvin reached up, and Katie stood up and helped him to his feet. He groaned and leaned backward.

"Not bad." He ran his hands over his chest. "Not bad at all."

"Come on," Katie said. "We have a demon's ass to kick."

Calvin and Katie headed back toward the demon, firing shots to draw its attention away from the cops it was currently tormenting by the cars. Katie chuckled as Calvin bounced up and down, cracking his neck back and forth.

He was not ready to go down, nor would he ever do so without a fight.

"All right, you bitch-assed punk!" Calvin yelled. "Thought you could get rid of me, huh? Well, my friend, I have some news for you! It's gonna take a lot more than your punk ass and a rock to take me out of commission." Calvin got into preaching mode, "I don't give a *fuck* what you think you are here to do! I'm here to tell you that it's time to sit the fuck down and shut the hell up as we open an old-fashioned can of whup-ass!"

Katie pulled her sword out with her right hand and held her knife in her left.

Slowly she started to walk toward the demon, bobbing and weaving as she approached him with an evil smirk on her face.

She was tired of being pushed around by this thing. It was time for him to step up or go the hell back where he came from.

Dodging a swipe of his claws, she sliced across his ankle with the sword, laughing and running around to the other side as he reached down and grabbed his ankle with a screech.

"Aw, did that hurt?" Katie made a pouty face. "Poor little demon baby."

She charged when his attention shifted due to a high-velocity round of some sort hitting him in the head. She leapt and stabbed him in the neck with her knife, pulling it back out as she dropped back to the ground, her eyes wide with excitement.

The demon screamed in pain and grabbed the wound as the magic of Katie's blade burned through him like the fire that raged on the outside. Before he could react, she slashed his knee with her sword and skipped backward, taunting him again.

"What's wrong?" She laughed. "Does that feel like hell and fire all wrapped up in a single stab?"

"I will crush you," he growled, holding his neck, his eyes red with fury and damnation.

"I don't know about that," Katie retorted. "You seem to be having a rough go at it. Do you need a timeout? Maybe a minute to gather those tears I think I see starting to fall down your face?"

Don't try this kindergarten bullshit with a higher-level

demon, but this guy? Go ahead—steal his lunch money. He has the emotional resilience of a two-year-old.

The beast growled and lunged at her, but she dodged to the side and sliced his other ankle. He roared in pain and tripped, taking out a mausoleum and at least three headstones as he toppled to the ground.

Katie risked a smile at Calvin, who just shook his head as he limped away.

He shook his head. "Always playin'."

"Come on, big-ass goon," Pandora taunted, speaking through Katie. "I've seen you in hell, so I know how tiny and weak you really are. There's no way you are going to beat these humans. You will fail at this, just like you did the last time. Oh, and way worse than the time you tried to hook up with me. I *know* you didn't think I would be interested in that tiny-ass dick."

"You bitch," the demon growled. "Your brother will come for you, and when he does he will not only kill that stupid bitch you are riding around in, but he will send you so far into the depths of hell it will take you centuries to make your way back out."

Sounds like a nice hiking vacation, Pandora quipped. *Too bad he will keep* you *tied up for his own personal pleasure. You know how he likes a good torture on Tuesday nights...and every other night, for that matter.*

"He is coming, and you are not prepared. I can *see* it." The demon chuckled evilly as he maneuvered himself around. "No matter what you say to me, it does not take away from the fact that he is going to crush you like ants. This is *his* planet now, and you are powerless to stop him."

"I feel like you have a bit of a crush on my brother."

Pandora/Katie laughed. "Does he know this? I mean he is as free and open as the rest of us, but I'm pretty sure he takes his sex with chicks. I mean, I don't want to break your heart, but there's no chance for the two of you. Sorry to be the bearer of bad news."

"Enough, you stupid witch," the demon snarled. "Are we going to end this, or do I need to just go ahead and step on you to put you out of my misery?"

"I don't like feet," Pandora/Katie replied. "I never did. I mean, to each his own. Everybody got a thang, but your foot fetish is really not my forte."

Katie watched as the demon stood back up. He was tired enough now that he wasn't on fire anymore—he wasn't wasting his energy like that at this point. Before he could get his footing she moved forward and leapt high enough into the air from the damaged mausoleum to grab the demon by the face and plunge her sword into his shoulder.

The demon screamed in pain and swiped across his face, sending Katie plummeting down to the ground. Her back cracked over a pile of stones and rubble.

She couldn't move.

I got this, Pandora said, starting to heal her.

You might want to hurry up, Katie moaned, watching the demon pull the sword out and throw it to the side.

As Calvin ran forward he took out his new short sword and, slowing down, jammed it into the beast's thigh. He pulled it right back out as the demon knocked him over. Calvin slid backward, grabbing his chest and wincing as he slowly worked to get himself back up and into the fight.

The beast hobbled slightly, but kept moving toward Katie.

Okay, go! Pandora shouted.

Katie rolled over and got up, rolling her shoulders and grimacing.

Nice work, she admitted.

I know. Pandora chuckled.

Katie met the demon head-on, pulling a gun out and firing it into his face as she jumped over the arm he swiped at her.

She grabbed a small piece of his barely-there clothing and used it to swing around his body, then pressed the barrel of her gun into his stomach hard and fired several rounds into him.

This time they pierced his skin, but it only slowed him down for a moment. Katie bitched and grabbed a reload when the gun just clicked.

Watch out, Pandora yelled, taking control of her body and hurling her to the ground.

The beast swung hard but missed, knocking Calvin, who had just gotten back into the fight, from his feet.

He slid backward through the grass, rolling over several times before his back jammed into a stone wall.

Katie looked over her shoulder at Calvin and growled, tired of the demon trying to kill her friend. They were both battered and bruised to hell, but the fight was nowhere near over.

This beast had to be taken down for good. Katie didn't want to fight him again if she could help it. She pushed away from the demon and stood up, slotting her pistols into their holsters and picking up her sword from the ground.

She wobbled back and forth while Pandora frantically scanned her body and tried to heal her as fast as she could.

The demon laughed. "Give up, little human, and maybe T'Chezz will have mercy on you." He considered his statement before adding, "But probably not."

"Not even in your wildest wet dreams," Katie/Pandora growled, red flashing in her eyes.

22

The fight continued, hit after hit, wound after wound, healing after healing.

Katie stopped attacking for a few moments and leaned against a statue, hiding and trying to gather her strength.

Her body was covered in blood, and this time most of it was her own. She looked at the wall Calvin had landed against a few moments before, but he was nowhere in sight.

She hoped that Eric had gotten him out of there. One more blow, and he would surely be dead.

She shook her head, completely out of breath and almost tapped out from the amount of stress she had put her human body through. Pandora could heal her over and over, but eventually there would become a point where she just couldn't take it anymore.

You are running low, Pandora admitted. *But so is he.*

MICHAEL TODD

This needs to end. Katie panted as she spoke. *And it needs to end now, before anyone else dies.*

Including us, Pandora stated.

Agreed.

Katie took a deep breath and stepped out from behind the statue. The demon was licking his wounds, keeping one eye out for the next attack.

He straightened up and balled his fists, chest heaving, body injured and torn. Katie limped forward carrying her sword, staring up into the demon's eyes.

No words needed to be said; they both knew they were down to one last battle. One or both of them would fall, but it had to be finished—neither had anything left.

The demon stepped forward and bent down, roaring loudly, and sending spit flying everywhere.

Pandora bitched, *Damn, a little Listerine would go a long way.*

Katie tipped her head back and let out her own warcry, raising her sword high.

The dawn sunlight glistened off the metal as she lowered it and readied herself for the attack.

They began to circle each other, moving in tune with each other's steps and carefully planning their next move. Just as Katie was about to charge shots rang out again, this time spraying bullets all over the beast's torso. Katie's eyes glistening as she glanced at Eric, who was holding Calvin up and walking slowly toward them.

"Come on, you limp-dick motherfucker," Calvin yelled, firing at the demon again. "You want to show me who's boss? You want to have a dick-measuring contest? I

216

promise you, my huge cock will win every single mother-fucking time."

Katie smiled and shook her head as he moved closer, firing bullet after bullet. The demon was weak; he could barely fight back anymore.

The beast backed up slowly, swatting at the bullets that stung his skin as blood splashed from the entry points. His skin wasn't nearly as tough as it had been at the beginning of the fight.

She sheathed her sword and stepped back, watching the demon grumble and grasp for a break in the fire.

When Calvin's automatic weapon ran out he threw it to the side and pulled his pistol out, stopping a moment. Eric still held him up.

Calvin fired the pistol at the demon's face and hit him in the cheek, then the ear, and then right between the eyes. A viscous black droplet of blood bubbled up where the bullet had entered, and the demon lifted his hand to rub it away.

His eyes were still red, but the end of the battle showed on his face. Katie was taken back at the heroic nature that Calvin displayed in the face of something so permanent, so *finite* as death.

Her pride surging through every vein in her body like an uncontrollable fire.

This was a new kind of intensity. A desire...no, a *need* to take this demon's life.

Katie needed to do it for herself, but she also needed to do it for Calvin. If he died, Calvin would see the demon go down before he did.

She needed him to see that he was a hero, that he was a

better man than that demon could ever be. She moved over to Calvin and pushed the barrel of his clicking pistol toward the ground.

"You did well, my friend," Katie told him softly.

"And I look good doing it, even half-dead." He chuckled, keeping his eyes on the demon, who was panting too.

She smiled. "Hell yeah, you do."

He looked at her for a moment, a smirk moving over his lips before his eyes drooped and fatigue washed over his face.

"Finish this," he requested quietly. "I want to go home."

"You got it." She nodded, unbuckling her vest.

Wait, what are you doing? Pandora squawked. *Pick up your knives! You need those knives!*

She dropped the vest on the ground and winked to Calvin, who just shook his head. She knew he thought she was nuts, but that didn't mean he didn't trust that she knew what she was doing.

Katie turned back toward the beast and took off, gaining speed as she dodged the rocks and ruts in the ground.

Fuck, Katie, Pandora screamed. *You are insane! You are going to get us both killed. Go back and get your fucking knives!*

Katie jumped from stone to stone and launched herself at the demon, hands outstretched.

She landed on his chest and held on tightly as he tried to look at her. The heat from his skin surged through her body.

Her destiny was at her fingertips. At that moment she looked up with a glint in her eyes. She tuned out the screams around her, the growls of the demon she was perched on, and the voice of the demon bitching endlessly inside her. As she reached back, the tired muscles in her arms shook wildly.

She thrust her arm forward, fingers transforming into a demon's claws.

She jammed her long talons into the beast's chest, feeling the hot blood pour over her skin as she pulled them back out. He screamed and writhed, pulling at his chest. He dropped to his knees for a moment and Katie slid down, then kicked off the ground and his leg to propel her body up and over his shoulder. She pushed her claws into his back and let go.

When he arched his back high into the air she slid to the ground, not waiting for his next move. Katie moved in front of the demon, kicking off his calf and up to his head to slash him hard across the face. The layers of black skin peeled back, and dark black blood dripped onto the grass and sizzled below the beast.

Katie jumped off him again and somersaulted to stand back up, watching him writhing in agony while holding the wounds she had just inflicted.

Pandora was silent, and so was the air around her. Her talons were even stronger and more powerful than her special blades, or any other weapon she had ever used on a demon.

Previously, demons had only reacted this way to pain not caused by her knives when Pandora pulled them from their human capsules and sent them straight back to hell.

Pandora must have worked through Katie to make her aware of the possibility and give her the use of her claws to defeat this disgusting beast once and for all.

The demon made its way back to its feet, where it wobbled back and forth. Katie breathed heavily, opening and closed her claws and staring up at the creature. It stumbled backward but caught its balance, now holding the wound in its chest.

"You still haven't had enough?" Katie ground out. "*We* are the inhabitants of this beautiful planet, not you. You are just a filthy fucking demon that is unknown to us, and when something unknown and dangerous attacks this planet *we* make sure it dies here." She spat on the ground. "You are no exception."

The demon laughed loudly, then wheezed for air.

"You stupid little bitch! You can kill me as many times as you want," he taunted, his voice patchy, "but in the end T'Chezz will come for *you*." He waved his hand toward the cops. "For *all* of you, and *you* will watch every single one of your friends die an agonizing death. Mark my words: this will never be over." He hissed, *"Never!"*

"You want to bet?" Katie growled, moving forward.

She slashed her claws across his calves and he fell to the ground, his head bobbing back and forth. She jumped on top of him and climbed onto his chest, from which perch she stared into his red eyes and smiled.

"Your kind will never win," she whispered as she glared down at him. She could tell he was out of gas.

"Katie," Damian yelled, throwing her his cross.

She reached toward the priest, her arm changing back to normal as she caught his cross and gripped it tightly in her palm. She slammed the golden object onto the beast's chest.

He screamed in pain and his flesh sizzled and melted as

she pushed it harder into his skin. She had to hold on and dodge his arms and fists as he thrashed around.

She gritted her teeth and shoved, visions of Calvin, the dead gangsters, the dead cops, and so many others flashing through her head. She screamed, matching his shrieks as she dug the cross into his chest cavity.

"What is T'Chezz's plan? Tell me!" Pandora/Katie screamed. "It is not too late. You are going to be gone for a long-assed time. Tell me where his plans lead!"

The beast screeched louder, fire bursting from his fingertips. Katie could barely hear Pandora screaming for answers; trying to get something—*anything*—out of the beast's thoughts.

Her rage had taken over, and she was out of control. She gripped the cross firmly in her hand, staring at the demon's face as he groaned and growled his pain.

"Tell her," Katie screamed.

"Who brought you back?" Pandora asked. "Who is here, and where is he? Is he here? In LA? Goddamn it, Barro, tell me something!"

Katie could tell the beast could barely think, much less answer questions. She pulled the cross halfway out and held it next to his barely beating black heart. She breathed deeply in anger, wanting answers but wanting revenge so much more.

"You are going to die," Katie growled. "Tell her what she wants to know and I will end your agony."

"You…" the demon spluttered, "are *all* going to die."

Katie snarled as the beast ran his eyes over her and opened them in surprise, then fear.

"Wh-wh-what are you?" the demon choked out.

"Your worst nightmare," Katie growled, shoving the cross back into his chest.

The beast's head flew back, and his arms fell to his sides. Fire shot from his eyes and mouth, shooting straight up toward the sky. Katie pulled her hand from his chest and stood over him, watching the life leave his ugly and battered body. Without warning he burst into flames, engulfing both him and Katie.

Everyone in cemetery went silent and Damian's eyes grew wide, watching the ball of flame in front of him. There was no sign of Katie.

The fire burned brightly for several minutes, visible from the sky as another police helicopter circled around, lighting up the morning dew on the cemetery below.

The pilot and copilot searched the ground, looking for any sign of the girl who had finished the beast, but the fire was too high and too hot for him to get a good look.

"The beast is on fire," the pilot reported into his headset. "I'm swinging around to take another look for the girl."

He turned the chopper in circles to get a better look at what was going on. Other police helicopters kept news choppers away from the conflagration.

There was an explosion where the demon had been, and a huge ball of fire and debris blew past the chopper.

He steadied the bird, breathing heavily and blinking wildly to adjust his eyesight.

"*Explosion!* There has been an explosion," the pilot

shouted. "Repeat, there has been an explosion. Waiting for the smoke to clear."

The pilot hovered over the spot where the demon had been, continuing to shine his spotlight downward. He looked down, swiveling his head back and forth to see if the demon was still there.

As the smoke began to clear, he pulled the mic to his lips.

"The area is clear." He sighed. "The demon is gone."

"Good work," the recipient replied. "Go ahead and get out of there."

"Hold on." The pilot leaned forward and moved the chopper to the side. "There is a body down there."

He shined his spotlight onto the ground where the demon had been, and gaped as he stared.

Katie was looking around in confusion, her face dark with soot. She breathed deeply and looked up, red-eyed, at the helicopter. He moved his light over her.

"The woman—the D Squad woman? She's alive," he said in wonder.

Katie put her arm up to block the searchlight and slowly reached up to flip him off.

"What's she doing?" the dispatcher asked.

"Well, she's flipping me the bird." He chuckled. "Let me pull back a little."

"There's something on the ground," the copilot said, pointing down. "Pull up more...I can't make out what it is."

The chopper moved higher, the beam of light widening to cover the entire space where the demon had died.

"What the fuck?" the copilot murmured.

There was a pentagram encased in a circle on the

ground around Katie, burned deep into the grass and soil. Small fires still blazed along the circle's edges. Katie was standing right in the center of it.

"It's a… We have a pentagram," the pilot reported. "On the ground where the demon died, surrounding the woman."

As if Katie could hear them her head shot up and she stared into the light with her bright-red eyes. The pilot grasped the stick tighter, feeling the entire helicopter shimmy and shake around him.

The copilot looked at the readings and then back at the pilot. "What's going on?" he yelled. "The readings are fine."

The pilot looked at him with wide eyes and then peered at Katie, who stood, fists balled and eyes red, staring angrily up at the helicopter. The spotlight burst and everything went black, sparks falling into the smoke-shrouded cemetery.

The pilot put the bird into a hover and looked at the copilot.

"I…uh… I think that is good enough for this morning," he said with a nod of his head.

"Yeah," the copilot said, staring down at Katie's shadow. "I don't think she liked the light whatsoever."

23

The scene was damned hard to believe.

Smoke billowed over the last remnants of the Inglewood Park Cemetery. Crushed stone was strewn all around the grounds, and police officers covered the remains of their fallen comrades as well as the other victims of the scene.

They couldn't confirm due to the smoke, but word was that the demon was gone.

Still the cops waited, their guns ready as they eyed the smoke.

While they had no idea what might come through that cloud—nor could their shocked minds take in everything that they just had witnessed—they weren't backing down.

Never in the history of humanity had a scene like that been witnessed by so many uninfected by the curse of the Damned.

"Someone's coming through," one of the officers

shouted, and over a dozen nearby officers' heads swiveled toward the voice.

Through the smoke and debris three figures slowly appeared. Eric and Damian supported Calvin as he limped past the smoldering embers, coughing and wincing at the pain.

A moment behind them strode the woman, her skin darkened from the ash and the red dissipating from her eyes.

The three men stopped and looked around at the ravaged landscape. The chopper in the background was unusable, and, not happy with taking it out of the sky, at some point the demon had chucked another rock at it.

That machine would never fly again.

Calvin looked over his shoulder at Katie's expression-less face and the smoke still coming off her skin. He didn't know how she had survived, but he knew where his faith would be placed from this moment on. He turned his head back around and eyed the cops, who slowly lowered their weapons as the Damned moved forward.

Damian looked at his male teammates and back at Katie before stopping once more.

Calvin recognized the three cops in front of them from the gun store. Their arms were crossed over their chests, and there were smiles on their faces.

"Friends of yours?" Damian asked, looking at Calvin.

"Something like that." Calvin chuckled, limping forward with Eric under his arm helping him remain upright.

"That was quite a show," one of the cops exclaimed.

"Fireworks and everything," the second added.

"It's good to see you still standing," the third told them, reaching out to shake Calvin's free hand.

"Kind of standing." He winced and pulled his hand across his ribs. "We might need a ride."

"We kept her safe." The first cop winked and the three parted to allow the men to view what was behind them.

It was their SUV—a little dusty, but not a scratch on her.

Calvin chuckled and nodded at the cops in thanks. Eric helped Calvin climb over the smashed cop car.

Damian turned and stuck his hand out to help Katie over. She grinned slightly, breaking the gravity of the scene —at least on her part.

She nodded at the three cops, who took a step back but politely returned her smile.

Everyone had seen what had happened, but none of them could explain why she was still alive, or what she *was*, exactly. They had seen the claws, the red eyes, the healing —everything—but nothing topped the ball of fire she walked out of unscathed.

At that moment she didn't understand it either, so she couldn't provide any guidance to the those staring at her.

Katie climbed into the car and reached back to squeeze Calvin's hand as Eric helped buckle him in. He looked at her with respect laced with something else; something she hadn't felt before.

She turned back to the front and pulled her brows together. Something vibrated in her back pocket, and she pulled out her phone to find a text from an unknown number.

It's me, where are you guys? Oh—this is Charlotte

Meet us in Las Vegas if you can, Katie texted back.

CU THERE, she replied, which made Katie chuckle.

Yeah, see you there, she thought to herself.

They left the cemetery after Damian confirmed he was the point of contact for the police until Calvin was capable of answering questions. Otherwise, the officers could and should talk to Korbin.

They went back to the hotel to shower and collect Calvin and Katie's things.

The guys led her in through the back, as to not draw any more attention than they already had.

She wasn't in any shape to go walking through the hotel. Neither was Calvin, for that matter. Damian stood guard outside her room, nodding as she went inside. She had to admit that a hot shower had rarely felt this good before. Her major wounds had healed, though her back was still sore.

She was just tired now, and given the complete lack of any comments Katie thought Pandora was as well.

After the showers and collection of their luggage the four Damned made their way back to the SUV and headed toward the airport, where the plane was ready to take them home.

Damian had already updated Korbin on almost everything, or at least what he needed to know at that moment.

On the way to LAX they stopped back at Randy's Donuts for some more sugary goodness. This time, though, Katie and Pandora were quiet.

Everyone grabbed some donuts, Katie deciding on half a dozen of her own.

They all sat around the table eating; not really talking, simply being there with each other.

The exhaustion was mental as well as physical. Calvin, they suspected, would need further medical treatment as soon as he got back.

When Katie was done, she wiped her hands and put her napkin on the table. Damian sat back and watched her, wondering what was going on in her head.

She seemed different, but he couldn't put his finger on what exactly it was.

Slowly she got up from the table and slinked backward, almost as if she were trying to leave unseen.

He watched carefully as Katie walked outside and to the left, where a homeless man was sitting with his back pressed against the window.

Damian observed as she talked to him with a smile on her face like he hadn't seen at all during that trip.

She bent down next to him and continued to chat, putting her hand on his shoulder and running it across his back. He couldn't tell what they were talking about, but the man seemed completely at ease. There was no fear at all in his face.

Damian tilted his head and sipped his coffee, just watching her kindness toward a perfect stranger—something he didn't see often from her. She was usually shy and standoffish if something wasn't part of the norm, like she had been when she had first met Mamacita's girls.

Damian looked back at Eric and Calvin, who were

talking about the demon attack and laughing at the comments Calvin had spat at the demon about his dick.

Damian shook his head, having missed that part since he had protected the pilot of their helicopter during the siege.

Calvin, Damian admitted, had been a real hero. He hadn't given up or backed away from the fight. He'd just kept going back in. Damian couldn't help but wonder if he too had gotten a little help from his demon, especially since the red ring in his eyes was just a bit brighter than normal.

He shook his head and looked back at Katie, who was now standing up straight as she listened intently to the homeless man speak.

She looked content, but at the same time there was something about the way she was standing that made him slightly suspicious. Her legs were shoulder width apart, and her hand rested on the butt of her weapon. Then it happened—something he wasn't expecting to see. Katie bent forward, still talking to the man, and pulled a demon right out of his back. The demon wriggled and squirmed, hissing and spitting in Katie's direction. It was still only an apparition, which made it look more like a ghost than a demon, but nonetheless she had seen it when no one else had.

Damian turned toward her slightly in his chair as she continued to talk, holding the demon higher and away from the man as he sipped his coffee. He seemed to come alive: his shoulders relaxed, his demeanor changed, and his back straightened.

He shook his head, not even believing what he was

watching. He glanced at the others, but they weren't paying any attention. Still holding the screaming entity in her right hand, Katie pulled some cash from her pocket with her left hand and handed it to the homeless man. He looked up at Katie with tears in his eyes, and stood up quicker than Damian thought an old man like him could have managed. He hugged Katie tightly, and a smile moved across her face as the demon in her hand squirmed, hissed, and growled behind the man's back.

There had been so many battles, and so much grief and anguish since the team had met Katie.

When she had first joined them she hadn't known how to fight, much less walk up to someone and pull a demon from his body. Now she did it with such finesse that unless you knew what to look for, you wouldn't have noticed at all.

Her demon had either taught her many new things—or had taken just a little more of her soul.

Either way Katie had come up a step, perhaps more so than Korbin himself. She was capable of handling what came at her now, no matter how big or scary. She always seemed to be on top of it, and at the same time managed to focus and help her teammates stay safe.

Damian noticed the appreciation in Calvin's eyes when he looked at her.

He knew Calvin was still alive because of Katie and whatever had happened in that cemetery before he and Eric had arrived. Damian sighed as Katie waved to the homeless man, who walked away. That smile on her face, however, faded quickly, and she jerked around and held the demon up in the air. He could see her talking to it, her eyes narrowed, as the beast cowered in her hands. No one else had noticed any of it yet, not even Katie's exit. No one but a Damned could have seen the apparition, but even so, no one seemed to notice the human standing right there in broad daylight giving the thing its Miranda rights.

Damian smirked. "You have the right to remain in hell. Should you choose to give up this right, I'll kill you to send your scrawny ass back down there…"

Wouldn't that be a lark? The Miranda Rights as rewritten by the Damned.

With a flash of her eyes, the demon disappeared. She dropped her hand to her side, surreptitiously wiping it on her jeans while looking down the street. She smiled and looked up as a plane flew overhead out of Damian's line of sight, rattling the glass windows.

She was in her own little world, protecting these humans with everything in her—even when she was so beaten down she should have been just relaxing and regrouping.

In that moment she reminded Damian of Korbin, not so much in skill, but the idea that work never ended. There was never a pause in taking care of the innocent. She always did what was necessary, what was needed, and what was asked of her, even if she did it on her own terms.

There was a lot to explain to Korbin for sure, but there was definitely something to be gained from her new abilities and the way she protected those around her.

Just then she turned and reached for the door. Damian turned back to the table and sipped his coffee, not wanting to make her feel uncomfortable.

She yawned as she walked past the guys and up to the takeout window.

He pushed a donut into his mouth and looked down at the table, listening to her order another chocolate-covered morsel of deliciousness and a cup of tea. He smiled at the tea part, glad to confirm that Katie was still in there.

She waited at the counter for a minute, smiling at the woman before she made her way back to the table. She sat down next to Damian and grinned bashfully.

"I thought you couldn't eat one more donut." Damian raised an eyebrow and looked at the item in question.

"For the right reason I can shove another one down," she replied, not giving any more answer than that.

He wondered if she knew he had seen her; if she knew that he had watched her amazing kindness.

He wondered how much of that was Pandora and how much was her, especially since her talents had quickly grown by what seemed like leaps and bounds. One thing he didn't wonder, however, was if Katie was still Katie, because through the red haze he could still see her just as brightly.

"You saved a lot of lives this morning," Damian said, lifting his cup. "Korbin is impressed, the police are impressed, and those that don't even know, they thank you too."

"It's my job," she said, taking a bite of the donut. "It is expected of me, and if I have the ability to do it, then that is exactly what I'll do every single time."

"You have really grown into the new you." Damian took a sip of his coffee. "I'm proud of you. You may be headed for a whole lot of demon shit in the future, but just know that you are admired and looked up to by this team. They feel safe when they are with you."

"They're not, though." She sighed as she interrupted him. "None of us are truly safe in battle, and that is a good thing, actually. It reduces the comfort level, and makes everyone stay on their toes."

"Very true." He nodded in agreement. "Will you be happy to get back to Vegas?"

"I will be." Katie sighed. "I need another hot bath and a nap and some more really good Italian food, not necessarily in that order. Though I have to say, this time I won't eat quite as much Italian food."

"Probably a good idea." Damian pursed his lips. "I know that Korbin and the rest of the team will be happy to have you back."

"Yeah, and we can work on my training," Calvin interjected, leaning his head into the conversation.

"After you get better," Katie told him, as if she were a mom.

"I'm good," he argued, giving her the shit-eating grin of a guy who is bullshitting.

"Oh yeah? Raise your arm above your head." Katie waved at him. "Go ahead."

Calvin scoffed and scooted back in his chair slowly. He lifted his left arm into the air, biting down on his bottom lip. Katie saw it start to shake almost immediately.

"And now the other one," she challenged.

"Yeah, no. I can't do it." Calvin laughed, lowering his arm. "All right…get better, *then* train. Hope you're happy."

"I am." She nodded and finished her donut. "Just another day in our lives, right?"

24

The plane ride back to Vegas was quick, but Katie was still glad to have some time to herself.

Pretty much everyone but her passed out as soon as the plane got into the air. She just wanted to stare at the passing clouds and relax back into her life once more.

The trip had been exhausting both mentally and physically. She had found herself in an unfamiliar position, so full of rage and anger that she could barely contain herself.

Katie finally broke the silence. *How did I survive that?* she asked Pandora.

What? The whole trip, or the giant fireball? the demon countered.

Both, but let's start with the fireball, Katie clarified.

I protected you, Pandora told her. *Well, it wasn't just me... It was you too, but I can withstand fire so I took you over until the fire was gone.*

What do you mean, "it wasn't just you?" Katie asked.

It's not really that important, Pandora responded. *You should just relax and not think.*

Okay, something is definitely up. Since when do you want me to relax?

I'm tired too, you know, Pandora huffed.

All right, Katie replied slowly, not really believing her. *Relax, then. I'll shut up—for now.*

Finally! Pandora exclaimed, with fake exasperation in her voice.

Katie smiled and leaned her head against her window, watching the clouds pass above her.

By the time they landed in Vegas she was feeling more like herself again. They made their way back to the base, where Korbin, Derek, and Jeremy were ready, beers in hand, to celebrate their victory and them returning in one piece.

Well, mostly in one piece.

Korbin nodded at Katie as she walked in and she smiled at him, knowing she would probably be summoned for a conversation sometime in the near future. But for now, it was all happy-happy and laughter.

Calvin had to skip the first part, since he was sent to the med bay to be completely checked over by one of the team doctors, who had come to their place just for that purpose.

Calvin had been beaten up and smashed and tossed around like a ragdoll during that battle, but amazingly enough, he was still standing. He was in much better shape than he had any right to be, when for all intents and purposes he should have been dead.

He knew he had come out of that when he probably shouldn't have, and a lot of that had to do with the demon inside him.

Calvin can't go back out right away, Pandora mentioned during the celebration. *Unfortunately, nothing but medicine and rest can help him at this point. His demon did the best he could, I can tell. He fixed him up enough to save his life, but beyond that the thing was completely baffled by what he should do next. Luckily what he did was enough, though I have to say that if he had taken a bullet there would have been nothing the demon could have done. He just isn't that skilled.*

Could you fix a bullet for me? Katie asked.

Most likely, Pandora replied.

What makes you so different? Katie wondered.

Level of power, I suppose, Pandora answered. *Ain't everyone me, baby.*

Pandora, Katie continued, unable to find a laugh. *I don't think I'm ready for your brother. You said that demon wasn't near his strength.*

No, he wasn't, Pandora agreed.

He almost killed me, Katie admitted. *My back still hurts where you repaired my spine. I would have died right then and there, not to mention the thousand other times throughout last night. If he had been any stronger, I am pretty sure I wouldn't have made it. That last blow, that last showdown—everything in me wanted to quit. It was literally the last bit of juice I had in me.*

Okay. Pandora wanted to scratch an itch that had been bothering her since the showdown. *Why didn't you pull your knives? I mean, it was the stupidest thing I have ever seen in my entire life. I thought we were both done for, that you were trying* to Hulk Hogan-wrestle a demon back into hell. And I'm sorry, honey, but you are not that strong—not even with my help.

Katie chuckled. *Because I have been wondering for quite a while why your people don't use weapons to kill each other? I mean, I can't remember a time I ever saw a demon with a weapon, not in any of the battles. They always come as they are, and go down without any type of weapon. If they had weapons it would make things a lot easier for them—not that I am suggesting a change in your people's methods. Anyway, my logical assumption was that you are your own personal weapon. Like your claws—they must do the job. I know you guys kill each other, so that isn't a question.*

Yeah. Pandora laughed. *I think we kill each other more than we kill other people. Of course, when we kill each other it just shoves us down in hell a little farther, and a powerful demon like my brother? He would be gone long enough that his ability to keep control would break. It could take him centuries to climb back to his present position. I think that's why we keep killing each other—we never fully get that satisfaction. When a human kills another human in this world, they never have to look at those dead-assed faces again. In our world, it's only a matter of time. That's why I don't get why my brother is trying so desperately to send me into the depths of hell. Even if he is successful, I'll still come back up and curse him out as I shove a red-hot poker up his ass and send him down for a while himself. There has to be some kind of final death, but I'm just not sure what it is yet.*

I would not want to be there when that happened if you can come back, Katie replied. *I can't imagine there is much shopping in the depths of hell. I can totally see you being more than pissed when you came back up.*

Last time I nearly decapitated him, she confided. *I was planning to set his head on my mantle with its mouth taped shut for a few centuries.*

You guys need family counseling. Katie giggled, putting a hand over her mouth.

Had it...he ate the counselor. She chuckled. *Right out of her damn chair. It was a real shame.*

You guys are unreal, Katie replied. *I'm glad I was an only child.*

There was a pause in their talk before Pandora broke the silence. *I have to tell you something, Katie,* Pandora whispered.

Yes? Katie asked.

I *didn't change your hands...*

"She is going to have a tough time with this conversation." Calvin said to Katie, "so try to be nice."

"What?" Katie sat back, looking at Calvin, hurt in her eyes. "I *am* nice."

"Yeah," Calvin replied. He stood up when Charlotte came into Bootlegger.

"You look tired." Calvin showed Charlotte to the table.

"It's been a long week." She sighed, sitting down and scooching over a bit in the booth. "This is a great restaurant, by the way. I ate here last time I was in Vegas."

"Yeah, apparently Katie likes coming back to the scene of the crime." Calvin chuckled.

"What crime?" Charlotte looked back and forth between the two of them.

"Nothing," Katie replied before Calvin could chime in. "I just really like the food here, and sometimes I have to overcome my weaknesses before I can move on. Apparently Calvin is perfect."

"It's about time you noticed," Calvin replied, rubbing her shoulder. "I thought I was going to go the rest of my life without someone paying attention and providing a qualified opinion about my perfection."

"If you aren't careful, I'll make that time really short," Katie replied with a smile.

"You guys act like siblings," Charlotte cut in, watching them.

"We are family." Calvin shrugged.

"That must be nice." Charlotte smiled. "My publication is a whorehouse of people just trying to get featured, and my real family isn't much to speak of either. That's why Aunt Chloe was so important."

"I'm sorry." Katie winced slightly. "My real family was just my mother."

"Not me." Calvin rolled his eyes. "I had the biggest family on the planet."

"Well, now that I am facing my weakness," Katie said, opening the menu. "I have to decide what I want to get."

The only weakness is your body, Pandora quipped. *And pain is weakness leaving that body, so the more in pain you get the stronger we both become. I suggest the ravioli and the steak.*

Katie ordered the steak and left it at that, deciding that Pandora's sighs could be dealt with later. There was no way she was eating that much in front of Calvin and Charlotte. It was bad enough that the waitresses and bartender remembered her from last time and were standing around to find out what she was going to order.

"So," Calvin began, "tell us what you found out."

Charlotte took a bite of the little bread squares and wiped her fingers on her table napkin. "Well, I went into that pawn shop and was able to look at the video footage," she told them. "I saw the guy's face, but didn't' recognize him right away. I was walking past a news stand the next day, though, and there that asshole was, smiling for the camera. He is a Los Angeles politician, specifically a Democratic senator. He is known for his sideways politics. He gives the public what they want, as long as his hand is in that cookie jar too."

"Like every other politician in the world," Katie said, rolling her eyes.

And in hell, because there are a lot of them down there, Pandora added.

"So here are the screenshots from the video footage, and this is the picture from the paper," Charlotte said, laying them out on the table. "His name is Senator Woodruff. Community favorite, made his way up from the slums. A real rags-to-riches story."

"Gee, I wonder how that happened," Katie snarked.

"Yeah," Charlotte said. "Anyway, this is your guy. And after this last demon attack, it only solidifies that more since it was in LA and he is from there."

"You did really great work," Calvin said.

"Oh, and I sent the camera," Katie said.

"I got it." Charlotte nodded. "Thanks a lot."

"So," Calvin said, folding his hands in front of him on

the table, "here is my side of the deal. On our team, I am the second. I take control if Korbin dies or becomes incapacitated. Now, along with that duty, I am also entrusted with the relationships across all the mercenary teams. That means I know everyone on every team, especially the team seconds. I've been speaking with someone since we made this deal, and I asked that person some very pointed questions so they would understand the severity of what we were trying to make happen. Charlotte, this is *not* a normal circumstance, and if it hadn't been so serious we would have laughed and walked away or just lied and told you that we had no idea what you were talking about. This isn't a game, though. There are people's lives at risk, and like we've been trying to tell you with your stories, if those lives are put out there to the public, they become more at risk."

"I understand," Charlotte said. "I mean, I think I do."

"What he is trying to say is, you need to keep your mouth shut," Katie added while eating a breadstick.

"Be nice," Calvin growled.

"What? I am." Katie shrugged. "You are a guy, so I'm going to tell it to her straight. I'm all for girl power, but I will power my girlie foot up your ass, Charlotte, if you talk about this stuff. *Capiche?*"

"Now," Calvin continued, ignoring Katie, "everyone in this risks getting caught breaking some very serious, very dangerous rules. You, my dear, are the one with the most to lose in this whole deal, because if you say anything—accident or not—you will have your mind wiped. That means you will have to start over in your career…everything. Are you sure you are willing to risk that?"

The reporter took a deep breath as tears slowly made their way down her face and nodded.

Katie looked at her strangely, since she had forgotten what it was like to have a really good cry. Calvin noticed her expression and elbowed her in the side. He reached into his jacket pocket and pulled out a generic burner phone and hit the speed dial for the team second of Hudson's Hitmen, then lifted the phone to his ear and waited.

"Hey, it's Calvin from Korbin's," he said. "Can you put Chloe on the phone? I have someone here who really would like to speak to her."

Calvin nodded his head in response to some question they couldn't hear. "Yeah, I got it." He passed the phone to Charlotte.

She just held the phone for a minute waiting for Chloe to answer, then tears started streaming down her face. Katie handed her a napkin and awkwardly patted her on the shoulder.

"Aunt Chloe?" Charlotte whispered, looking down at the table.

Calvin looked at Katie with pride, puffing out his chest. Katie didn't know if it was Pandora or what, but her only response was a small smile and a roll of her eyes. She got excited, though, when her food was set down in front of her.

Maybe she needed to work on her social skills a little bit more for the future.

Calvin leaned over and spoke in her ear. "I know you are hungry, but you aren't reacting like a human with a heart at the moment."

When dinner was over, Calvin covered the tab and Charlotte thanked them over and over for letting her talk to Chloe. She knew she would probably never see her again, but just knowing she was safe and she was alive made Charlotte feel a hell of a lot better—and not so alone anymore. That was one thing Katie could relate with, not feeling alone anymore.

They walked out the door together before going their separate ways.

Just then, Pandora popped into her head like clockwork.

That reporter, as sweet and disgusting as that scene just was, ruined my dinner, Pandora bitched.

How? We ate, Katie told her, striding to the SUV and opening the door.

We ate a steak, she stated, *when we could have spent the entire evening stuffing you full of food again. Seriously, that is like the best place ever. We could have had another all-night food fest.*

Well, I'm telling you right now that I'm not overeating another damn thing until you explain why my new bras are already too tight, Katie barked. *Like, we just got these damn things. You promised me when we gorged on donuts that you would only work on muscle, not curves.*

I did only work on the muscle, Pandora protested.

Why do I not believe you? Katie asked suspiciously.

Hey, breasts have muscles too, she said innocently.

Oh. My. God, Katie growled. *You made my breast muscles larger?*

Yeah. You said muscles, so I took the leftover protein and calories and built your pecs up. She snickered. *Voila! Big beautiful boobies which don't need a bra.*

Never say that again, Katie said, slamming her door. Never!

Which part? Pandora wondered. *Big? Beautiful? Boobies? Or no bra?*

Five minutes later Katie responded, *BIG, you slut!*
Oh.

25

Things had finally gotten back to normal around the base.

Everyone was training on a daily basis, the intel was flowing in steadily, and Katie seemed to be back to her old self once more.

When Damian got back he'd had a long, extensive talk with Korbin about what had happened in the cemetery that night, and Korbin had told him he needed some time to think about everything.

He didn't call Katie in or let her know that he knew, just took time to think about what the next steps might be and what he was supposed to do with the information.

After dinner that night, Damian wandered around the complex, trying to find Korbin. Surprisingly enough, he wasn't in his office or the office at the company next door, either. Damian checked his room and the chapel, but still no sign of Korbin.

Finally he decided to go up to the roof, and he found

him up there. He was sipping scotch while lounging on a chaise and contemplatively watching the sun drop behind the mountains.

It was clear from the scotch and the look on his face that he was thinking about more than swords and weapons. His mind was obviously clouded with a million other things—and it made Damian a little nervous, since he was there to talk further about Katie and what Korbin believed would be the best course of action.

Damian felt like he had become Katie's protector, in a way.

"Hey, boss." Damian plopped down in the chair next to Korbin.

"We don't use this roof enough," Korbin remarked, looking at his glass as he swirled the amber liquid. "We spent the money to decorate it. It looks really nice and the view is killer, but no one ever comes up here to enjoy it. I sure as hell don't."

"I remember when we decorated it." Damian chuckled. "We were so confused about what the hell the decorator meant by 'stucco.'"

"I thought it was some kind of cake." Korbin shrugged and took a sip. "I went to every baker in the city trying find it."

"Who knew it was just a strange paint?" Damian laughed.

"Painting technique," Korbin corrected.

"Ah yes, technique." Damian nodded.

Korbin looked at Damian. "You want some?"

"Sure," Damian said, watching him pour three fingers of Glenlivet into a Glencarin whiskey glass. "Fancy glass."

"You like those? They were the higher-ups' Christmas present to me last year." He chuckled. "Obviously they don't know me in the least. I once drank homemade whiskey from a tin cup in the middle of the desert. I'm not picky about my drinkware."

"That sounds dangerous," Damian commented.

"The tin cup or the whiskey?" Korbin asked.

"The sand," Damian clarified. "You don't take to the sun really well. I remember the pool party last year. You ended up looking like a freaking lobster."

"Oh, God, that was miserable." He chuckled. "I couldn't sit down for a week. Anyway, what brings you up to the roof tonight?"

"I was looking for you," he replied. "I wanted to find out if you had come to a decision."

Korbin took a sip of his scotch and leaned his head back, watching the last of the sun dip below the horizon. He sat there quietly for several moments, just thinking.

Damian sipped his drink and glanced around as he waited for his boss to reply. Finally, he pursed his lips and looked at Korbin.

"Without faith," Korbin began, "Humanity will fail. That is not a question or a maybe, it is an absolute. And I don't necessarily mean faith in a higher being, though there is nothing wrong with that. What I am talking about is faith in people, in yourself, in the truth, and in the hard choices. Without that faith, humanity doesn't stand a chance in the future."

"I agree." Damian smiled.

Korbin looked at Damian. "I just hope that my faith is not misplaced."

"It isn't," Damian replied.

"How do you know?" Korbin probed.

"Because," Damian looked into Korbin's eyes, "no demon in control of a body would touch that cross, and Katie didn't hesitate." He waved a hand, slicing the air. "Not for a second. She might be Damned, but she isn't *lost*, Korbin."

"I really hope you're correct." He sighed. "Otherwise the humanity is as good as gone. You know that, right? That if Katie is gone and we let her demon lead us down a path to extinction it will be our fault, and our asses that have to raise their hands and say 'our bad!'"

Damian chuckled. "I don't take blame. It's your decision." Damian smiled as took a sip of his whisky. "I don't get paid the big bucks. Besides, I don't think she would lead us to extinction, just pain and suffering, that's all."

"You're not making me feel better about this." Korbin smiled tightly.

"You've made the right choice." Damian reached over and patted Korbin on the shoulder. "Trust me."

It was night. A rather quiet one, but the streets were busy as usual. A woman, tall and pretty but with a certain stare that could stop anyone in their tracks, walked intently through the rough part of the city.

The gangs were always in the streets and didn't like it too much when anyone was on their turf, but for her they made an exception. For her they created a wide walkway, kept their eyes to themselves, and not a single one of those thugs catcalled, whistled, or even thought about touching her.

Her heels clacked against the sidewalk as she walked with purpose toward a meeting that she was already five minutes late for.

She reached an intersection and looked down at the paper in her hand and then back up at the signs. She turned left and picked up her pace, almost jogging toward the bright club lights on the next street over.

There were people lined up out the door, wearing skimpy dresses and the newest jeans and ready to party. As she passed the line she stopped and stared at a guy who had been stupid enough to whistle at her.

He smiled at first, but as he stared her in the eyes his smile quickly faded away and a look of fear crossed his face. She chuckled and rolled her eyes before continuing toward the door.

As much as she wanted to put him in his place, she didn't have time for that—not that night.

The doorman looked her up and down, not sure who she was. Carefully the woman leaned forward and whispered something in his ear. His face went white and he stood up straight, shaking his head and ushering her through the door.

He pointed to the back where two guards were standing. The woman winked at him, brushing off the coat check as she made her way into the club. The music was loud and electronic, and the bass bumped so hard her teeth rattled in her head.

She had never liked clubs. They were too crowded and too expensive, and if she wanted a sweaty man to rub himself all over her she could just go to the male strip club on the other side of the town and pay fifty bucks.

Most of the women in there gave her a onceover and went back to their conversations, while most of the men stopped and stared at her as she made her way through the crowd.

She was beautiful, sure, but it was her eyes that made them stare—something she had come to really like in recent days.

There was no better way to get someone's attention than by flashing the red demon eyes. The smell of booze wafted into her nose and she crinkled it; no time to even think about relaxing and enjoying some whiskey. She was on a mission—one that required her entire attention, and one she did not want to screw up.

After several pushes, an ass-grab where she put the guy on the ground, and a drink spill she managed to dodge, the woman made it to the other side of the club.

Two guards stood in front of a large ornate door. The woman stretched up and whispered into one of their ears, and the guy—about a foot taller and a hundred pounds heavier—nodded and stepped to the side, opening the door. The woman smiled and nodded as she stepped through the doorway into a nicely decorated room that looked like it belonged in an Asian mob house.

Not in the back of a skanky club.

As soon as the door was shut behind her, the music faded and she was able to hear herself think again.

She pulled on the edge of her skirt and took a deep breath, feeling a little out of it after running down the street and then fighting through the mob of desperate clubgoers. When she had straightened herself out, the woman looked up at another guy, who held open a curtain and welcomed her into the next room. The woman smiled and followed him through the curtain to where an Asian woman in a very pretty green dress was waiting for her.

She smiled at the Asian woman, thinking how elegant she looked in that dress and how her hair reminded her of the fifties, or at least movies about the fifties.

She was too young to remember anything other than the nineties. The woman stood up and held out her hand, offering the seat across from her. She nodded and took the seat.

"Miss…"

"Just call me Mia," the Asian woman said.

"'Mia,'" the woman said. "Thank you for seeing me. I am sorry I am late. Business was…busier than normal."

"Not a problem." She smiled and nodded to the table in front of her. "Tea?"

"Oh, yes please," the woman said, turning over her cup.

Mia served the tea with an air of confidence. She passed the sugar and cream and sat back in the chair, crossing her legs. The woman smiled, feeling the confidence in the woman and knowing she thought she was in complete control of the situation.

"Your club is…nice," the woman began.

"Thank you," Mia replied. "I have owned it for ten years. The secret to it is having security you can trust, employees you can trust, and police you can trust." She winked. "It's really all about trust."

"It's just a front though, right?" the woman asked.

"You are a smart woman." Mia laughed. "Most clubs are

a front for something or other, whether its simple tax evasion or mobster activity. I can promise, though, that we are neither. You know what service I provide, so I suppose I would need a front for that. It's not the most legal matter."

"Of course not," the woman said. She leaned forward, took off her sunglasses, and flashed her eyes.

Mia's smile faded and she shook, spilling some of her tea on the saucer. She stared at the woman, realizing that she was no longer in charge. In fact, she was no longer in a situation she was comfortable being in.

She looked around for her security.

"They won't be needed." The woman reclined in her seat, taking the cup with her. "I am not here for you, just the service you provide."

"Of course," Mia said, bowing her head. "I am honored to have someone of your stature here with me tonight. Had I known you were coming—or that it was *you* that was coming—I would have made sure to have you escorted back."

"That would have been nice." The woman stared at her.

"Right," Mia said. "Let me just get the documents."

Mia stood up and walked over to a small stand with a large wooden box sitting on top. She slowly opened the lid and retrieved a leather satchel from inside.

She hurried back to the table and looked to the side, nodding at her service staff. The girl rushed over and took the tea and tray from the table before disappearing into the back room. The woman smiled at the fear in everyone's eyes.

Mia pulled a stack of paper from the satchel. "Here are

the documents for your new identity: your birth certifi-
cate, Social Security card, driver's license with a number
that is attached to the DMV in case you get pulled over, a
passport where you just need to add the picture, and the
credit card you requested in your new identity."

"Thank you." The woman checked each piece carefully
before looking up. "And none of these will fail me?"

"No, they are all registered to the correct places," Mia
explained. "That is why we charge what we do. They are
not fake ID documents, they are legitimate identities."

The woman smiled. "Wonderful. Will I need anything
else?"

"No. Now that you have all of it you will be able to get a
replacement license, buy a home, go to Brazil—whatever
you wish to do," Mia told her. "Of course, we ask that you
promise anonymity if for any reason you are caught."

"Of course," the woman assured her. "My lips are
sealed."

The woman stood up and opened her purse, pulling out
a large envelope and laying it on the table. Mia shook her
head and piled the documents back into the leather satchel,
which she handed to her. The woman bowed slightly and
smiled.

"Fifty thousand, right?" she confirmed

"Yes, thank you." Mia bowed her head.

"It was a pleasure having tea with you," the woman said.
"May I ask what kind of tea that is?"

"It is a family blend," Mia answered. "A mix of greens
and herbals—something my mother used to make to calm
us and get us to bed at night. I find that it helps relax two
strangers when they are meeting for the first time."

"I can see where that might be useful." The woman smiled. "I love tea. All kinds, really, but mostly I drink Chai or English Breakfast."

"Chai is one of my favorites." Mia smiled nervously. "Though I must confess, I don't like making it, since it's very time-consuming."

"Yes," the woman agreed. "Well, thank you."

"May I just ask one question?" Mia inquired, stopping the woman.

"Yes?" She kept her face toward the door.

"Why did you want a new identity?"

A smile moved over her face as she turned around and looked Mia in the eyes.

"I want a damned car of my own," Katie said with a wink before placing her sunglasses back on her face.

First, THANK YOU for not only reading this story, but checking out our Author notes here in the back, as well!

I would tell you what Laurie has been up to the last week, but then I might take away some of her thunder (or admit knowledge she is hiding? Hmmmm....)

So, I'll let her divulge her <redacted> that got caught up in a <redacted> situation with Amazon that made her want to <redacted> her hair all out.

And her Christmas Cookie adventure on Youtube. I'll speak to this story and what we are doing!

Loraine (Cover artist)

So, Laurie was wanting cover artist(s) for the 7Sons project we started together. Part of my responsibility was finding additional cover artists. LMBPN Publishing (my company) already had 3 artists working with us monthly, another two on project by project basis and we were looking to bring out 56 more books.

No way I could use our existing artists...*No freaking way!*

So, time to figure out how to find another GOOD artist.

Now, I happened to accomplish this task. I found three awesome artists, one (Loraine) that I'm trying to keep tied up (not literally...figuratively... she's in South Africa so it can't be literal no matter how business savvy that decision might be – you know, chained to her computer working on covers? No? Must be me.) The second I grabbed for a twelve book commission and a third I'd love to work with, but should wouldn't commit for so many books and we (my company) can't commit for fewer.

Oh well, life happens.

Anyway, I get in touch w/ Loraine and then I get on a video call with her. She had two (2) clients at the time, but I am trying to explain "I'm someone you will want to work with, give me a shot!"

While I'm a 'big name' in Indie writing circles, that really doesn't mean much to most people, including those who make covers for a living. So, when an author – completely out of the blue – contacts you from the USA when you live in South Africa claiming he wants a 12 book contract?

Yeah, I imagine she could be doubtful. So, I did something that would cause her to *believe*.

I told her to bill me half up front for the first 12 covers (and she did, no hesitation on her part...oh no.)

However, when the money showed up, I become a real client.

Since Laurie was out of commission at the beginning (the reason I went looking for Loraine in the first place) I engaged Loraine on a couple of projects.

The first was a skunkworks project for the Tales of the Wellspring Knight, she blew PJ Cherubino out of the water.

Then, she did the cover art for my proof of concept with Jude's first 3D model of a character and *WE HAD SOMETHING!* Now, Jude rocked our fourth cover's model (for SIT DOWN, SHUT UP and PULL THE TRIGGER) in a day I think, and as soon as I have the hi-res, I'll be able to toss it to Loraine who will have something back to me in about a day as well. I can't explain how nice it is to be able to find a pose, send it to Jude and in 48 hours have a model review to look at.

Unfortunately, Laurie is about to unleash the beast of 56 covers and I am going to have to share Loraine's time.

DAMN!

I asked Loraine how she got involved in doing covers and here is her answer (I asked for 'short.' Seems I get what I ask for (she did ask me if I needed more, but we are trying to get this book out tonight.)

FROM LORAINE:

I started on Photoshop years ago, in 2010 when I was staying abroad in Ireland for my gap year after matric, I was on holiday for basically the entire year, so I wrote a book and made my own cover.

That was about when I first started with photo manipulations on Photoshop.

Don't ask about the book, the publishers closed and sent my book back on a cd. I have no other version of it and I lost the cd a few years back when we moved around a lot.

I might rewrite it some day when I have time, but for now I'll stick to covers lol

Further, I studied graphic & advertising design when I got back in South Africa in 2011, but it did not cover Photoshop.

Everything I know about PS was self-taught.

WELCOME LORAINE!

WHAT IS YOUR DAMNED (Katie) SCHEDULE?

The future....Ahhhh, the future.

So, SIT DOWN, SHUT UP and PULL THE TRIGGER (PBTD 04) is due out on Monday, April 2nd (2018) and then, we are looking to produce 2 books a month'ish for the next 4 months. Due to a NEW series coming out, and my Kurtherian Book PAYBACK IS A BITCH, we have a stutter step in May where we are writing 2 books, but only 1 book will come out.

However, in June we should have THREE released to make up for May. Tentative Dates are:

APRIL 2nd, 13th, 27th

MAY 18th

JUNE 1st, 15th, 29th

WHAT THE HELL ELSE ARE YOU DOING?

Oriceran... And *Mr. Brownstone...*

About one year ago this time (2017), I wrote a 2,000 word scene with 'a guy' that kick started the whole Oriceran Universe. But, I was writing Kurtherian Gambit and could not spend the time to make the series – Martha Carr came to my rescue.

However, I've made it back… And my guy is coming alive.

That guy's name is James Brownstone, and he is already a badass. A bounty hunter who works the tough jobs, bringing home the money, and listens to BarBQ shows and podcasts and drives around in a nicely kept up Ford F-350 that can't be hacked by all of the technology and magic easily.

You know, a simple life and he likes it that way.

Life, however, is not about simple and two females came into his nice, organized (and simple) life.

One is a young teenage girl that helps find his dog but her mother has disappeared, *taken*. The other is a tomb raider who has a hidden past.

Neither relationship is straightforward nor simple.

All hell breaks loose, and James has to learn to handle life when feelings he has not had to deal with intrude in his KISS (Keep It Simple, Stupid) mantra.

I'm LOVING these stories, and I hope many of you will check them out. The first one is: FEARED BY HELL - The Unbelievable Mr. Brownstone Book 01 and the release schedule is:

APRIL 6th - FEARED BY HELL – Book 01

APRIL 20th – REJECTED BY HEAVEN – Book 02

MAY 3rd – EYE FOR AN EYE – Book 03

MAY 25th – BRING THE PAIN – Book 04

We will have an additional two series associated with this one. The first series is about Shay, the Tomb Raider with the hidden past and her books start arriving at end of April.

The third series is about Allison's life at The School of Necessary Magic. We do not have a release schedule for that series, *yet*.

MORE PROTECTED BY THE DAMNED

So, I was video conferencing with Laurie a couple of nights ago discussing the amazing success this series has garnered, and the fans who enjoy our concepts.

We have tentatively agreed to greenlight our next one to two series in the PBTD Universe, and I will be setting up characters in the next month or so, for possible releases in June timeframe. If you are happy to keep reading additional characters and character arcs (I'm thinking our next 'contestant' is going to be a lady's player with a succubus – or my second thought below.)

He wants girls...She wants guys. What could possibly go wrong with that?

Another relationship is the totally screwed up person with an OCD demon... because, who doesn't want a girl who just wants her beauty sleep and do nothing in her life to deal with a demon that has her day all planned out...

To the second?

Imagine how frustrated the demon is going to be?

Susie rolled over in bed, pulling a pillow over her head to block out the morning light. "You think you are going to get me to do shit my parents worked 22 years to accomplish, but failed? You are out of your damned demon mind.... So, fuck off and let me sleep."

C'lechtock (now Timmons for whatever fucking reason Susie called him that) pursed his lips inside her body, then started playing with her gastro-intestinal tract.

Seems last night she was eating beans, and then followed her dinner with a Coke Float and Butterfingers...

All the right ingredients to make this a place she will not want to smell in about twenty minutes.

She will get up, oh...she will indeed or his name isn't...

Fucking Timmons.

If you have possible ideas, PLEASE jump into the Facebook Group and let's discuss them! These ideas above are just working concepts right now. If better suggestions happen, we can push them back.

LMBPN WELCOMES YOU INTO OUR FAMILY OF STORIES...

I hope you stay awhile ;-)

Ad Aeternitatem,

Michael Anderle

AUTHOR NOTES - LAURIE STARKEY

MARCH 24, 2018

What a friggiddy fracking jacked-up insane asylum sort of week! *pulls hair and dances like a goon from Fraggle Rock* Whew. Okay. Now that THAT's over... Let me tell you about it.

As I mentioned in my last author note, we decided to take our Texas country-asses up to Washington D.C. for the cherry blossom festival. We wanted to see the flowers and tour the monuments over a seven-day period, but boy, were we in for a surprise.

Something like a Nor-easter rolled in on Day Two. We were out, running through the rain (looking like wet mole-rats) and yet, still trying to keep the positive, upbeat parental persona for the twelve-year-old bopping along with us.

It was FREEZING. By the time we got back home, we were beat. And it had started snowing. Like–hellacious snowing.

I'm from Texas. We don't get snow. The cold rain melts

long before it hits our humid-ass no-winter-having ground.

It didn't just snow. It SNOWED. All of you in the North East are like, "Right… and?"

Snowed and snowed and snowed. So, what did we do?

We decided to take a walk in it. *rolls eyes and shakes head* And we got a bit lost trying to find a coffee shop. We were trying to be hip, but that didn't exactly pay off. We get to the Starbucks finally, and I've got no feeling in my fingers, toes, the last half of my ass… it was rough.

And the damn Starbucks is closed. Of course, it is.

My husband and I just stood there, looking homeless. People passed by, giving us a concerned look and asking, "Starbucks is closed?" heard that fifteen times.

"Um, no. We're just waiting on a formal invitation from the barista. YES. It's closed. Hello. Shitburgers."

So anyway, in other news, I released/launched 3 books since I left Texas 10 days ago. Two with Mike on this project, which were super smooth, and one for my Weston Parker romance line, which was a fucking nightmare from the bowels of the devil's crotch. (I might exaggerate from time to time, but this isn't one of those times.)

We loaded the romance book on Saturday, and this one was a sweet romance. I've written some "sexy, your mother better not read this" books, but this one wasn't one of those. So, we check later that night (Saturday night), and the book has been pushed into the erotica category. Now, that would be fine if it was an erotica story, but it wasn't.

Erotica fans everywhere would have read that book and used it as kindling later that night, thinking someone from preparatory school wrote it. Sweet. Love. Story.

So, that resulted in six days of fighting with Amazon. Why did I fight? Because you don't get some of the advertising and NO promotion value from Amazon if you're in the erotica category. I got three emails back from them, telling me that we were out of the wrong category, but were we? Hell to the no.

It was the longest week of my life. By the time I finally got on the phone with someone, I was in tears. We'd spent so much money and time trying to advertise the book, and Amazon tied my hands. I rarely cry, but boy did that poor lady get it.

Thirty days of my life writing the book, paying for everything, as well as my team of seven people editing, proofing, promoting, graphics, ads…. You name it, and we do it for that romance line.

And finally, last night, the clouds parted and it all cleared up. I'm happy to say we're number sixty-four in the top 100 paid overall on Amazon as I type this, which honestly seemed like an insane possibility, but we did it. My team is thrilled, and I am insanely relieved.

In other news, that convo that Mike mentioned above has so many possibilities for spin offs from Protected by the Damned, as well as a few new series that we had a good time kicking around.

It's always a bad idea to get me and Mike in a room together, on a call together, etc. We will come up with two million ways to tell more stories and start pushing them. My hubs was listening from the side, but he just nodded every time Mike and I came up with something new.

Someone needs to be there to say, "NO! You must sleep, eat and occasionally shit."

Ugh. Fine. Ha!

Thanks for reading this madness. I swear it just gets more and more mental every time I write one of these notes.

To the Protected by the Damned Facebook Group–you guys rock so much. Thanks for welcoming me into the fold. I appreciate that so much and love the energy you guys have. Makes me want to tell more stories and faster... just for you.

This note has gone on for damn near ever, and I'm in the backwoods of Tennessee, visiting some family as we drive home, so no internet. Not sure there's running water to be honest. Internet is NOT top priority right now. LOL.

I'll tell you about the cookie BS next time, and I'll even drop a link to the video of the cookie madness in the back of Book 4 for you. Not that you want to see it, but just in case someone is devastatingly bored, I'll hand it over.

Thank you. Thank you. Thank you. There is nothing more precious to a writer than to know he or she is affecting people with their craft. To know that some of you are laughing, shedding a tear, rereading the books and having fun? Priceless to us.

We will be bringing you more of what you love, and if we're not–someone mentioned pitchforks. I'm all for it. Bringing you books, not getting poked.

To you guys that read our stories, thank you. We do what we do for you.

Slave to many stories,

Laurie Starkey

CONNECT WITH MICHAEL TODD

Want more?

Find us On Facebook

https://www.facebook.com/Protected-by-the-Damned-193345908061855/

BOOKS BY MICHAEL TODD

PROTECTED BY THE DAMNED
Torn Asunder (01)
Killing Is My Business (02)
And Business Is Good (03)
Sit Down, Shut Up, And Pull The Trigger (Coming)

For a complete list of Michael's Kurtherian Gambit Universe books please click this link.

Kurtherian Gambit Series Titles Include:

FIRST ARC

Death Becomes Her (01) - Queen Bitch (02) - Love Lost (03) - Bite This (04) - Never Forsaken (05) - Under My Heel (06) - Kneel Or Die (07)

SECOND ARC

We Will Build (08) - It's Hell To Choose (09) - Release The Dogs of War (10) - Sued For Peace (11) - We Have Contact (12) - My Ride is a Bitch (13) - Don't Cross This Line (14)

THIRD ARC

Never Submit (15) - Never Surrender (16) - Forever Defend (17) - Might Makes Right (18) - Ahead Full (19) - Capture Death (20) - Life Goes On (21)

THE SECOND DARK AGES

with Ell Leigh Clarke

The Dark Messiah (01) - The Darkest Night (02) - Darkest Before The Dawn (03) - Dawn Arrives (04)

THE BORIS CHRONICLES
with Paul C. Middleton

<u>Evacuation</u> (01) - Retaliation (02) - Revelations (03) - Redemption (04)

RECLAIMING HONOR
with Justin Sloan

<u>Justice Is Calling</u> (01) - Claimed By Honor (02) - Judgement Has Fallen (03) - Angel of Reckoning (04) - Born Into Flames (05) - Defending The Lost (06) - Saved By Valor (07) - Return of Victory (08)

THE ETHERIC ACADEMY
with TS Paul

<u>ALPHA CLASS</u> (01) - ALPHA CLASS: Engineering (02)

TERRY HENRY "TH" WALTON CHRONICLES
with Craig Martelle

<u>Nomad Found</u> (01) - Nomad Redeemed (02) - Nomad Unleashed (03) - Nomad Supreme (04) - Nomad's Fury (05) - Nomad's Justice (06) - Nomad Avenged (07) - Nomad Mortis (08) - Nomad's Force (09) - Nomad's Galaxy (10)

TRIALS AND TRIBULATIONS
with Natalie Grey

<u>Risk Be Damned</u> (01) - Damned to Hell (02)

~THE AGE OF MAGIC~

THE RISE OF MAGIC

with CM Raymond and LE Barbant

Restriction (01) - Reawakening (02) - Rebellion (03) - Revolution (04) - Unlawful Passage (05) - Darkness Rises (06) - The Gods Beneath (07) - Reborn (08)

THE HIDDEN MAGIC CHRONICLES

with Justin Sloan

Shades of Light (01) - Shades of Dark (02) - Shades of Glory (03) - Shades of Justice (04)

STORMS OF MAGIC

with PT Hylton

Storm Raiders (01) - Storm Callers (02) - Storm Breakers (03) - Storm Warrior (04)

TALES OF THE FEISTY DRUID

with Candy Crum

The Arcadian Druid (01) - The Undying Illusionist (02) - The Frozen Wasteland (03) - The Deceiver (04) - The Lost (05) - The Damned (06)

PATH OF HEROES

with Brandon Barr

Rogue Mage (01)

A NEW DAWN

with Amy Hopkins

<u>Dawn of Destiny</u> (01) - Dawn of Darkness (02) - Dawn of Deliverance (03) - Dawn of Days (04) - Broken Skies (05)

TALES OF THE WELLSPRING KNIGHT
with P.J. Cherubino

<u>Knight's Creed</u> (01) - Knight's Struggle (02)

~THE AGE OF MADNESS~

LIVE FREE OR DIE
with Haley Lawson

Unleashing Madness (01)

~THE AGE OF EXPANSION~

THE ASCENSION MYTH
*with Ell Leigh Clarke *

<u>Awakened</u> (01) - Activated (02) - Called (03) - Sanctioned (04) - Rebirth (05) - Retribution (06) - Cloaked (07) - Bourne (08) - Committed (09)

CONFESSIONS OF A SPACE ANTHROPOLOGIST
with Ell Leigh Clarke

<u>Giles Kurns: Rogue Operator</u> (01) - Giles Kurns: Rogue Instigator (02)

THE UPRISE SAGA

with Amy Duboff

Covert Talents (01) - Endless Advance (02) - Veiled Designs (03) - Dark Rivals (04)

BAD COMPANY

with Craig Martelle

The Bad Company (01) - Blockade (02) - Price of Freedom (03)

THE GHOST SQUADRON

with Sarah Noffke and J.N. Chaney

Formation (01) - Exploration (02) - Evolution (03) - Degeneration (04) - Impersonation (05) - Recollection (06)

VALERIE'S ELITES

with Justin Sloan and PT Hylton

Valerie's Elites (01) - Death Defied (02) - Prime Enforcer (03)

SHADOW VANGUARD

with Tom Dublin

Gravity Storm (01)

ETHERIC ADVENTURES: ANNE AND JINX

with S.R. Russell

Etheric Recruit (01) - Etheric Researcher (02)

Other Books

with Craig Martelle & Justin Sloan

<u>Gateway to the Universe</u>

~THE REVELATIONS OF ORICERAN~

THE LEIRA CHRONICLES
with Martha Carr

<u>Waking Magic</u> (01) - Release of Magic (02) - Protection of Magic (03) - Rule of Magic (04) - Dealing in Magic (05) - Theft of Magic (06) - Enemies of Magic (07)

SHORT STORIES

You Don't Touch John's Cousin: Frank Kurns Stories of the UnknownWorld 01 (7.5)

Bitch's Night Out: Frank Kurns Stories of the UnknownWorld 02 (9.5)

with Natalie Grey

Bellatrix: Frank Kurns Stories of the Unknownworld 03 (13.25)

Challenges: Frank Kurns Stories of the Unknownworld 04

AudioBooks

Available at Audible.com and iTunes

CLICK HERE TO SEE ALL LMBPN BOOKS ON AUDIBLE

www.ingramcontent.com/pod-product-compliance
Lightning Source LLC
Chambersburg PA
CBHW050229110726
47898CB00007B/2078